The Path to the Spiders' Nests

Italo Calvino, one of Italy's foremost writers, was born in Cuba in 1923 and grew up in San Remo, Italy. When the Germans occupied northern Italy during the Second World War, he joined the partisans. The novel that resulted from this experience, published in English under the title *The Path to the Spiders' Nests*, won wide acclaim. Best known for his experimental masterpieces *Invisible Cities* and *If on a Winter's Night a Traveller*, Calvino was also a brilliant exponent of allegorical fantasy in such works as *The Castle of Crossed Destinies*, *The Complete Cosmicomics*, and the trilogy, *Our Ancestors*, comprising *The Cloven Viscount*, *The Baron in the Trees* and *The Non-Existent Knight*. An essayist, journalist and the author of many stories, Calvino won the prestigious Italian literary award, the Premio Feltrinelli, in 1973. Eighteen of his books have been published in English.

The *New Statesman* said, 'Calvino cannot be defined within our existing terms . . . his is a voice which cries out the need to rehabilitate ourselves to our books, our lives, our world' and *Time* called him 'Quite possibly the best Italian novelist alive, one of those storytellers who hold a mirror up to nature and then write about the mirror.'

Italo Calvino died in September 1985, aged sixty-two.

ITALO CALVINO

The Path to the Spiders' Nests

Translated from the Italian by Archibald Colquhoun
Revised by Martin McLaughlin

PENGUIN BOOKS

PENGUIN CLASSICS

Published by the Penguin Group
Penguin Books Ltd, 80 Strand, London WC2R ORL, England
Penguin Group (USA) Inc., 375 Hudson Street, New York, New York 10014, USA
Penguin Group (Canada), 90 Eglinton Avenue East, Suite 700, Toronto, Ontario, Canada M4P 2Y3
(a division of Pearson Penguin Canada Inc.)
Penguin Ireland, 25 St Stephen's Green, Dublin 2, Ireland (a division of Penguin Books Ltd)
Penguin Group (Australia), 250 Camberwell Road, Camberwell, Victoria 3124, Australia
(a division of Pearson Australia Group Pty Ltd)
Penguin Books India Pvt Ltd, 11 Community Centre, Panchsheel Park,
New Delhi – 110 017, India
Penguin Group (NZ), 67 Apollo Drive, Rosedale, North Shore 0632, New Zealand
(a division of Pearson New Zealand Ltd)
Penguin Books (South Africa) (Pty) Ltd, 24 Sturdee Avenue, Rosebank,
Johannesburg 2196, South Africa

Penguin Books Ltd, Registered Offices: 80 Strand, London WC2R ORL, England

www.penguin.com

First published in Great Britain by Jonathan Cape 1998
Published in Penguin Classics 2009

008

Originally published in Italy as *Il sentiero dei nidi di ragno* copyright © 1947 by Giulio Einaudi,
Editore, Torino. Original translation copyright © 1956 by William Collins & Sons Co. Ltd.,
London. Translation of Preface and revised translation of text copyright © 1998
by Martin McLaughlin
Copyright © The Estate of Italo Calvino, 2002
All rights reserved

The moral right of the translator has been asserted

Printed in England by Clays Ltd, Elcograf S.p.A.

978-0-141-18973-4

www.greenpenguin.co.uk

Note to the 1998 Translation

Italo Calvino (1923–85) wrote his first novel at the age of twenty-three, in a few weeks in December 1946. Published in October 1947, *The Path to the Spiders' Nests* won the Premio Riccione that year, and sold 6,000 copies, an unusually high level of sales for the time. But the author soon turned his back on his first book, as he modified his early neo-realist poetics, and refused to authorize a re-edition until 1954. Only a decade later, in 1964, as he prepared to abandon realism altogether and embark on the fictions that were to make him internationally famous, did Calvino go back to his first book and authorize a third, definitive edition; and this time, to accompany the novel, he composed a preface which remains his most substantial and revealing self-commentary, as well as an indispensable, objective analysis of Italian neo-realism.

Despite its length, however, the preface makes no explicit mention of the substantial changes that Calvino made in the text of both the 1954 and 1964 editions. In both cases he excised or toned down certain passages depicting Cousin's and Pin's anti-feminism, Mancino's political extremism, as well as some violent details. However, reading between the lines, we can see that sections two and three of the preface do at least hint at the changes, when he criticizes the youthful extremism of the novel in its exaggerated emphasis on sex, violence, political ideology, and expressionist characters, and then adds: 'The unease which this book caused me for so long has to a certain extent subsided, but to a certain extent still remains.' Only late in life and nearly twenty years after writing the preface did Calvino explicitly acknowledge the changes and their motivation. In an interview with students in 1983 he admitted:

> I had written things that seemed to me too brutal or exaggerated [in *The Path to the Spiders' Nests*]. So I tried to attenuate some of those overstated and certainly brutal passages, even although they were attributed to the thoughts of other characters, not to me. Perhaps it was also to do with the fact that, when I wrote the book, I imagined that it would be read by just a few hundred people, as happened at that time for works of Italian literature. Instead when I realized that its readership was so much more numerous, the novel's status changed in my own eyes. I reread it and thought 'How on earth could I have written such things?' So I made some corrections. Of course there are still exaggerated elements in the novel: these are due to the almost adolescent phase I was still undergoing when I wrote the book, a phase which young people go through. It is the book of a very young man.

The implications of this publishing background for the book's English translation are important. Since the first English version has a copyright of 1956, it is likely that the translator, Archibald Colquhoun, used the 1954 edition, but comparison of the passages omitted and added by the author at various stages suggests either that the 1954 copy used by the translator had somehow retained one or two passages from the first edition (such as the very different opening paragraphs), or that Colquhoun was given the 1947 text with cancellations and additions marked by the author. It is worth adding that Colquhoun himself or his publisher also censored certain passages deemed unsuitable for the sexual and political climate of the 1950s (such as the description of Mancino's obscene tattoos or the mention of the serenity of the Soviet Union).

The task of issuing an English version of *The Path to the Spiders' Nests* suitable for the 1990s meant that Colquhoun's translation had to be updated in at least three ways: first by cutting out passages which Calvino himself omitted for the definitive edition, especially as the preface alludes, however implicitly, to these excisions; secondly by inserting the sections that Calvino had added to produce the 1964 edition as well as those that had been silently censored in the English version; and thirdly to eliminate a number of errors that had crept into Colquhoun's otherwise fine translation. It was also necessary to update numerous words and turns of phrase which are now misleading or meaningless. These are the four main areas in which I have revised the 1956 translation. I have also altered Colquhoun's translation of the title from *The Path to the Nest of Spiders* to *The Path to the Spiders' Nests*, partly to be more faithful to the plural *nidi* in Italian, partly to avoid the inadvertent echo of 'a nest of vipers' in Colquhoun's title (which produces quite the wrong associations in English), but particularly because we know that Calvino was delighted that the novel's title in English could both be more concise and could avoid the awkward double genitive in Italian ('Il sentiero *dei* nidi *di* ragno'). Similarly, the important preface which had been translated in 1976 by William Weaver in a slightly abridged form now appears in English in full for the first time, though in this case rather than simply revising Weaver's translation I have translated it from scratch.

Readers often find prefaces off-putting, and either postpone reading them until after finishing the novel, or simply choose not to read them. However, the inclusion of Calvino's preface in this volume not only respects the definitive will of the author, it also provides the reader with a typical sample of Calvino's elegant essay-writing as well as a good novel. In fact, even allowing for the difference of genre between a literary preface and a novel, these two pieces of prose allow us a glimpse of how Calvino had matured as a writer in the two decades between the 1940s and the 1960s. The preface displays some typically Calvinian symmetries and dialectics. For a start, it has, in all, twelve sections like the twelve chapters of the novel. The first section deals with external elements of the context in which the book emerged (the anonymous oral tradition of narrative in post-war Italy as people were allowed to speak freely again and recount their adventures); the second with the book's Italian literary ancestry (Verga, Vittorini, Pavese). This dialectic between external and literary elements informs the whole preface: the next three sections return to non-literary factors (the question of commitment), while the two central ones establish international literary influences (Hemingway, Russian writers, Stevenson). Finally Calvino returns to other external factors (the discussions with 'Kim', his own meditations on violence, his identification with Pin), before concluding with further literary discussion (of Fenoglio and of the cost of writing one's first novel).

Salman Rushdie pointed out that *The Path to the Spiders' Nests* had one of the best titles in post-war literature, but felt that the ending had 'dipped its feet in slush'. But if the close of the novel is rather anodyne, the more mature preface ends with one of those elegant Calvinian paradoxes that are typical of the writer at the peak of his powers: 'A completed book will never compensate me for what I destroyed in writing it: namely that experience which if preserved throughout the years of my life might have helped to compose my last

4

book, and which in fact was sufficient only to write the first.' Reviewing Calvino's last work, *Mr Palomar*, the poet Seamus Heaney talked of the author's fondness for 'binary blarney' and noted that 'symmetries and arithmetic have always tempted Italo Calvino's imagination to grow flirtatious and to begin its fantastic display'. The reader can enjoy something of that love of binary systems and symmetries here, and can appreciate that even in this early novel and its 1964 preface Calvino is, in Heaney's words, 'on the high wire, on lines of thought strung out above the big international circus'.

Martin McLaughlin
Christ Church, Oxford

Preface to *The Path to the Spiders' Nests*

This is the first novel I wrote. I could almost say it was my very first piece of writing apart from a few short stories. How does it strike me when I look at it again today? Well, I read it now not so much as one of my own works but rather as a book which arose anonymously out of the general climate of the time, from a moral tension that was in the air, and a literary tendency which epitomized our generation immediately after the Second World War.

The literary explosion of those years in Italy was not so much an artistic phenomenon, more a physical, existential, collective need. We had come through the war, and those of us of the younger generation – who had just been old enough to be partisans – did not feel crushed or defeated or damaged by the experience; rather we were the victors, carried onward by the forward thrust of the battle which we had just won, the exclusive guardians of its legacy. This was not facile optimism, however, or gratuitous euphoria; quite the opposite: what we felt ourselves to be the heirs of, was a sense of life being something which could begin again from scratch, a feeling of public outrage against injustice, even a kind of flair for surviving danger and slaughter. But the accent that we put on all this was one of almost provocative cheerfulness. Many things grew out of that climate

7

including the tone of my earliest short stories and of my first novel.

This is what strikes me most today: the anonymous voice of that age, which comes across more strongly than my own individual inflections which were still rather uncertain. The fact of having emerged from an experience – a war, a civil war – which had spared no one, established an immediacy of communication between the writer and his public: we were face to face, on equal terms, bursting with stories to tell; everyone had experienced their own drama, had lived a chaotic, exciting, adventurous existence; we took the words from each other's mouths. The rebirth of freedom of speech manifested itself first and foremost in a craving to tell stories: in the trains that were starting to run again, crammed with people and bags of flour and drums of oil, every passenger would recount to complete strangers the adventures which had befallen him, as did everyone eating at the tables of the temporary soup-kitchens, every woman in the queues at the shops. The greyness of everyday life seemed something that belonged to another epoch; we existed in a multi-coloured world of stories.

The result was that those who began writing in that period found themselves dealing with the same subject matter as these anonymous storytellers: not only did we have the adventures that each one of us had endured personally or witnessed, but there were also tales which came to us already formed as narratives, with a voice, a cadence, a facial gesture to accompany them. During the partisan war the adventures which we had only just lived through were transformed and reshaped into stories told around the fire at night; they had already assumed a style, a language, a tone of bravado, which relished harrowing detail or horrific effects. The subject matter and language of some of my short stories, as well

8

as some parts of this novel stem from this newly born oral tradition.

And yet, and yet ... the secret heart of the way we wrote then lay not merely in this basic universality of content – that was not what really spurred us to write (perhaps the fact of having opened this preface with a re-evocation of a collective state of mind, makes me forget that I am talking about a book, written matter, lines of words on a blank page); on the contrary, it was as clear as day to us that the stories that were told were simply raw material: the explosive charge of freedom which inspired young writers in those days resided not so much in their urge to provide documentary information, as in the urge to *express*. Express what? Ourselves, life's rough taste which we had just experienced, the many things we thought we knew or were, and perhaps really did know and really were at that time. Characters, landscapes, shoot-outs, political messages, dialect words, swear-words, lyric passages, violence and sexual encounters, all these were but colours on our palette, notes on our scale: we knew only too well that what counted was the music not the libretto. We were all content-driven, yet there were never such obsessive formalists as ourselves; we claimed to be a school of objective writers, but there were never such effusive lyricists as us.

That was what 'Neo-realism' was for those of us who began writing in that context; and this book represents a typical sample of 'Neo-realism''s virtues and defects, arising as it did out of that naive desire to create literature characteristic of a 'school'. For the fact is that those who now think of 'Neo-realism' primarily as a contamination or coercion of literature by non-literary forces, are really shifting the terms of the question: in reality the non-literary elements were simply there, so solid and indisputable that they seemed to us to be completely natural; for us the problem appeared to be entirely

9

one of poetics, of how to transform that world which for us was *the* world into a work of literature.

'Neo-realism' was not a school. (Let me try to be precise about these matters.) It was many voices combined, mostly voices from the provinces, a many-sided revelation of the different Italys that existed, a revelation also – and in particular – of the Italys that had been least explored by literature. Without this variety of different Italys, each of them unknown to the other, or which we believed were unknown to each other, and without this range of dialects and local forms of Italian which were to be leavened and moulded by the literary language, 'Neo-realism' would never have existed. But it was not simply an updated version of nineteenth-century regional 'verismo'. The local settings were intended to give a flavour of authenticity to a fictional representation with which everyone the world over would be able to identify – like the American provinces in the works of those 1930s writers whose direct or indirect heirs so many critics accused us of being. That is why the language, style and rhythm of what we wrote had so much importance for us – for this realism we strove for, which was at the same time intended to be as far removed as possible from nineteenth-century naturalism. We thought of ourselves as descending from a line, or rather a triangle, of literary models – Giovanni Verga's *I Malavoglia (The House by the Medlar Tree)*, Elio Vittorini's *Conversazione in Sicilia (Conversation in Sicily)*, and Cesare Pavese's *Paesi tuoi (The Harvesters)* – which was to be the starting point for all of us, working with our own local lexis and landscape. (I am still talking in the plural as though I were referring to an organized, self-conscious movement, even now when I am trying to explain that it was just the opposite of that. How easy it is, once one starts talking about literature, and even in the middle of the

10

most serious, factual discussion, to slip unwittingly into telling stories ... That is why literary analysis, whether my own or anyone else's, annoys me more and more.)

My landscape was something which I jealously guarded as my own (this is where I could really begin this preface: by reducing to a minimum the above section on 'The autobiography of a literary generation', and plunging straight in to a discussion of what concerns me most directly, perhaps I can avoid generalizations and vagueness ...), a landscape which nobody had ever really written about. (Except the poet Eugenio Montale, and he was in any case from the other side of the Ligurian Riviera. I felt that I could almost always read Montale from this perspective of local memory, identifying both with his imagery and with his language.) I was from the Western Ligurian Riviera. In polemical spirit I obliterated the whole tourist coastline from the landscape of my home town, San Remo: the palm-fringed promenade, the Casino, the hotels and villas. It was almost as though I was ashamed of it. I began with the alleyways of the Old Town, went up along the hillside streams, avoiding the geometric fields of carnations: I preferred the terraced strips planted with vines and olives surrounded by crumbling, dry-stone walls. I advanced along the mule-tracks rising above the fallow fields up to where the pinewoods began, then the chestnut trees: that was how I moved from the sea – always seen from above, like a thin strip between two green curtains – up to the winding valleys of the Ligurian Pre-Alps.

I had my own landscape. But in order to represent it I had to make it take second place to something else, to people, to stories. The Resistance solved this problem of the fusion of landscape and characters. The novel which I would never have been able to write without that fusion is here. The everyday landscape of my whole existence up until that time had now become totally extraordinary and full of exciting incident. One

11

single story unwound from the gloomy alleyways bridged by arches between the houses in the Old Town all the way up to the woods, and it was the story of armed men chasing and hiding from each other. I was able to portray even the villas now that I had seen them requisitioned and metamorphosed into guardhouses and prisons, and the carnation fields too, once they had become dangerous open terrain, perilous to cross, evoking only the rattle of gun-fire in the air. It was from this new possibility of situating human stories in landscapes that 'Neo-realism' . . .

In this novel (I had better return to my topic: it is too early to start to rewrite the official apologia for 'Neo-realism'; nowadays I am more inclined to analyse the reasons for my abandonment of it) the signs of the literary age in which it was written are mixed up with the signs of the author's own callowness. The exaggerated emphasis on the themes of sex and violence ultimately seems rather naive (today's readers' palates now tolerate much spicier fare) and forced (the author's subsequent output confirms that these were alien and transient themes).

Equally naive and forced might appear the urge to graft an ideological message on to the story, particularly on to a story such as this which is set in a completely different key – that of immediate, objective narration both in terms of imagery and language. To satisfy this need for the ideological component, I adopted the expedient of concentrating all the theoretical considerations into a chapter which is different in tone from the others, Chapter IX, the one containing the reflections of the commissar Kim, which almost constitutes a preface inserted in the middle of the novel. My earliest readers all criticized this expedient and advised me to cut the chapter out completely; but despite realizing that it harmed the unity of the work (at that

12

time, stylistic uniformity was one of the few aesthetic criteria that we were sure of), I stood my ground: the book came out as it was, warts and all, with that hint of being something hybrid and artificial.

The other great subject of future critical discussions, the question of dialect versus standard Italian, was also in evidence here in its naive phase: dialect elements gathered together like patches of local colour (whereas in subsequent works I would try to absorb all these dialectal influences into the standard language, like a vital but hidden source of nourishment). The style was very uneven, at times bordering on the precious, at other times just written down as it came, aiming solely at immediacy of expression; it became a kind of documentary archive (including local sayings and songs) which bordered on folklore . . .

In addition (I shall continue with this list of signs of the novel's age, since a preface written today is only worthwhile if it adopts a critical stance), there was the manner of depicting characters: they all had exaggerated, grotesque features, twisted grimaces, dark, deep-rooted psychological scars. If Italian literature and art had missed out on expressionism after the First World War, it made up for it at the end of the Second. Perhaps the correct label for that artistic epoch in Italy ought to be 'Neo-expressionism' rather than 'Neo-realism'.

The distortions operated by the expressionist lens in this novel are projected on to the faces of those who had been my closest comrades. I was at pains to turn them into caricatures, to make them unrecognizable, 'negative', because I could write poetically only about 'negativity'. At the same time I felt remorse both because I knew that reality was so much more varied, more emotive and nuanced, and because I knew that the real people who were models for the characters were so much richer and better in human terms. This remorse was to stay with me for years . . .

This is the first novel I wrote. What effect does it have on me rereading it today? (Now I really have come to the point: this feeling of remorse. This is where my preface should begin.) The unease which this book caused me for so long has to a certain extent subsided, but to a certain extent still remains: it resides mainly in my relationship towards something so much bigger than myself, involving emotions which affected all my contemporaries – tragedies, acts of heroism and of generosity and ingenuity, as well as dark dramas of conscience. The Resistance: how does this book fit into 'the literature of the Resistance'? At the time when I wrote the book, the problem of creating a 'Resistance literature' was still an open one, and we all felt that there was an imperative on us to write 'the novel of the Resistance': in fact barely two months after the Liberation Vittorini's *Uomini e no (Men and Not Men)* was already in the bookshops, its main theme our central dialectic of death versus happiness. Milan's partisan groups thus already had their novel, full of fast action ranging over the concentric map of the city. Those of us who had been partisans in the mountains would have liked to have had our novel too, one that reflected our different rhythms of action, our more irregular comings and goings . . .

But I was not so culturally ill-informed as to be unaware that the influence of history on literature is indirect, slow and often contradictory. I knew perfectly well that many great historical events went by without inspiring any great novel, particularly so in 'the century of the novel' *par excellence*, the nineteenth century: I knew that the great novel of Italian Unification had never been written . . . We all knew that, we were not that naive, but I believe that when one has lived through a significant

14

historical epoch or taken an active part in momentous events, one feels a particular responsibility . . .

In my case, this responsibility made me feel in the end that the theme was too demanding and solemn for my abilities. Consequently, in order not to let myself be cowed by it, I decided to approach it not head on but obliquely. Everything had to be seen through the eyes of a child, in a world of urchins and no-hopers. I invented a story that would hover on the margins of the partisan war, tangential to its acts of heroism and sacrifice, but that would at the same time convey its colour, its rhythm, its bitter taste . . .

This is the first novel I wrote. How can I define it today, as I look at it again after so many years? (I have to start again from scratch. I was side-tracked and ended up showing that the book was born of a strategy aimed at evading commitment; whereas on the contrary . . .) I can define it as an example of 'committed literature' in the fullest and richest sense of the term. Nowadays when one talks about 'committed literature' one generally has a mistaken notion of the term, as though it were a kind of writing that is simply an illustration of a thesis already defined a priori, completely independently of any poetic qualities. Instead, what used to be called in French *engagement*, commitment, can come out at all sorts of different levels: here it is intended to emerge through the book's imagery and lexis, narrative drive, tone, style, nonchalance, challenge.

My choice of theme already suggests an element of bravado, of almost provocative challenge. But challenging whom? I would have to say that I wanted to conduct a campaign on two fronts simultaneously: to launch an attack both against the detractors of the Resistance and against the high-priests of a hagiographic Resistance that was all sweetness and light.

The first front: barely a year after the Liberation, 'bourgeois respectability' was already fully reinstated, and it exploited every socio-economic factor of that period – the excesses of post-war youth, the resurgence of crime, the problem of re-establishing respect for the law – in order to exclaim: 'See, we told you so all along, these partisans are all the same, don't let them come talking to us about the Resistance, we know full well what kind of ideals they had in mind . . .' It was in this climate that I wrote my book, in which I wanted to answer the bourgeoisie with a paradox: 'Okay, let's assume you're right: I'll portray not the best but the worst partisans imaginable. At the centre of my novel I will place a division entirely composed of characters who are slightly twisted. Now then, what's the difference? Even those who threw themselves into the struggle without really knowing why acted on an instinct based on human solidarity, – an urge which made them a hundred times better than you, and made them active participants in the course of history such as you will never be, even in your wildest dreams!' The significance of this polemic, this challenge is now rather remote from us: and even in those days, I have to admit, the book was read simply as a novel, and not as part of this debate about history's verdict on the Resistance. Nevertheless, if today the book still creates a little provocative frisson, then it stems from the polemic of those times.

Actually from the double polemic of those times. Even though the battle on the second front, the one inside 'left-wing culture', also seems rather distant. At that time the first attempts were just being made to give 'political direction' to literature: the writer was asked to create the 'positive hero', to provide images that were salutary and instructive in terms of social behaviour and revolutionary militancy. All that was just beginning, I said: and I have to add that here in Italy such pressures had very little influence or following even in subsequent years. Still, the danger that the new literature would be required to fulfil a celebratory and didactic function was in the air: when I wrote this book I had just noticed this, and my hackles were immediately raised, my claws unsheathed against any imposition of a new rhetoric. (In those days I still preserved intact my anti-conformist instinct, a legacy that is difficult to maintain, but which – even though it has on occasions been less prominent – is still a standby of mine, in this age which is so much more prosperous but no less dangerous . . .) My reaction then could be encapsulated in these words: 'Oh, so you want "the socialist hero" then? You want "romantic revolutionaries"? Well, I'm going to write you a story about partisans in which nobody is a hero, nobody has any class-consciousness. I'm going to portray the world of marginal people, the lumpenproletariat! (This was a new concept for me at the time, and I regarded it as a monumental discovery. I did not realize then that it had been and would continue to be the easiest material for fiction.) And the book will be the most positive and revolutionary work of all! What do we care about someone who is already a hero, someone who already has class-consciousness? What we ought to be portraying is the process by which those two goals are reached! As long as there exists a single person who does not have that awareness, our duty must be to concern ourselves solely with that person!'

That was the way I was thinking, and in this polemical rage I flung myself into the novel and distorted the faces and personalities of people who had been my closest comrades, people with whom for months on end I had shared a mess-tin of chestnuts and the risk of death, people for whose fate I had trembled, whose nonchalance in taking risks and whose totally unselfish way of living I had admired enormously. These were the characters whose features I turned into masks twisted by perpetual grimaces, into grotesque figures, and for whom I invented murky, shadowy pasts – or at least what in my

17

youthful naivety I thought murky, shadowy pasts must be like
... Only to be haunted by remorse for this for years ...

I have to begin the preface again from the start: I have not got it right yet. What I have said so far would make it seem that in setting out to write this book I had everything quite clear in my head: the polemical arguments, the opponents to defeat, the poetics to defend ... On the contrary, even if this was all there, it was still in a confused and shapeless state. In reality the book developed almost by chance: I had begun to write without a clear plot in mind, starting off from the urchin-boy character, that is to say from direct observation of reality – his way of moving, of talking, of relating to adults – and, as a narrative framework for him, I invented the story of the sister and the pistol stolen from the German. After that, his arrival among the partisans turned out to be a difficult transition: this shift from a picaresque story to an epic involving the whole populace threatened to destroy everything, so I had to create a device that would allow me to continue to maintain the story on the same level, so I invented the band of partisans under Dritto.

By this stage, as always happens, the story itself virtually imposed its own plot. But into this structure, into this outline which was developing almost spontaneously, I decanted my own still fresh experiences, a crowd of faces and voices (I distorted the faces and mutilated the characters, as writers always do since for them reality becomes like clay, a malleable medium, and they know that this is the only way they can write, and yet it causes them remorse ...), a flood of conversations as well as my own readings which blended in with those experiences.

What you read and what you experience in life are not two separate worlds, but one single cosmos. Every life-experience, in order to be interpreted properly, evokes certain things you

18

have read and blends into them. That books always derive from other books is a truth which is only apparently in contradiction with the other truth, that books derive from practical existence and from our relations with other people. Almost as soon as I had stopped being a partisan I discovered (initially in excerpts in magazines, then as a whole book) a novel about the Spanish civil war which Hemingway had written six or seven years previously, *For Whom the Bell Tolls*. It was the first book with which I as an ex-partisan could identify: it was from reading that novel that I began to transform into narrative motifs and phrases what I had seen and experienced, the detachment of Pablo and Pilar was 'our' detachment. (Nowadays that book of Hemingway's is the one which I probably like least; in fact Hemingway became the model for many of us only when we discovered his real stylistic mastery in other books of his, especially in his earliest short stories.)

The kind of literature we liked was that which contained this sense of a seething humanity, of ruthlessness, and also of nature. We also felt that the Russian writers of the civil war period – that is, before Soviet literature was purged and became idealized – were our contemporaries. In particular, Isaac Babel: his *Red Cavalry*, already translated into Italian before the war, and one of the masterpieces of twentieth-century realism, also sprang from an intellectual's encounter with revolutionary violence.

But also influential, though to a lesser extent, was Alexander Fadeyev (at least before he became a mere functionary of official Soviet literature). He had written his first book, *The Rout*, with that particular sincerity and vigour (though I do not remember whether I had already read it when I wrote my novel, and I am not going to check either: that's not important, since similar situations breed similar books in terms of structure and style). Fadeyev knew how to finish things as cleanly as he had begun them, as he was the only Stalinist writer, in 1956, who showed that he realized the extent of the tragedy for which he had been partly responsible (the tragedy in which Babel and so many other genuine writers of the Revolution had lost their lives). Refusing to go in for hypocritical recriminations, he faced up to the strictest consequence of his actions, and took a pistol to his forehead.

These books, then, form the background to *The Path to the Spiders' Nests*. But when you are young every new book you read is like a new eye which opens on to the world and which modifies the viewpoint of the other eyes or book-eyes which you had before, and so in the midst of this new idea of literature which I longed to create, there was also space for a revival of all the literary worlds which had captivated me from childhood onwards . . . The result was that while setting out to write something like Hemingway's *For Whom the Bell Tolls*, at the same time I also wanted to create a work akin to Stevenson's *Treasure Island*.

It was Cesare Pavese who understood this instantly: from his reading of *The Path* he intuited all my favourite literary texts. He even cited Ippolito Nievo, the nineteenth-century Italian writer to whom I had wanted to pay secret homage by basing Pin's meeting with Cousin on Carlino's encounter with Spaccafumo in Nievo's *Le confessioni di un Italiano* (*The Confessions of an Italian*).

It was Pavese who was the first to talk of a fairy-tale tone in my writing. Up until then I had not been aware of this, but from that point onwards I became only to conscious of it, and tried to confirm that definition. The story of my literary career was already beginning to be mapped out, and now I think I see it entirely encapsulated in that beginning.

Perhaps, in the end, it is only your first book that counts, perhaps you should only write that one and stop; you only make the great leap that one time, the opportunity to express your real self happens only once, what you have to say inside you is either said at that point or never more. Perhaps real poetry is possible only at one moment in your life, which for most people coincides with their earliest youth. Once that phase has passed, whether you have expressed yourself or not (and you won't know whether you have for a hundred, maybe a hundred and fifty years: contemporaries cannot be good judges), from that point on the die is cast, all you will do subsequently is imitate others or yourself, you won't ever manage to produce a single word that is authentic or unique . . .

I must digress here. Every discourse that is based on purely literary factors, if it is honest, ends up in this stalemate, this failure which writing always entails. Luckily, writing is not just a matter of literature, but of *something else*. Once more I need to alter the course this preface has taken.

This *something else*, as I thought then, was a definition of what the partisan war had been like. I and a friend of mine, a contemporary, who is now a doctor, and who was then a student like myself, used to spend the evenings in discussion. For both of us the Resistance had been the formative experience; for him in a much more demanding way than for me, since he had ended up with serious responsibilities: at barely twenty years of age he had become a commissar of a partisan division, the one to which I had belonged as a simple 'garibaldino' volunteer. In those days, just a few months after the Liberation, we felt that the way everyone talked of the Resistance was completely wrong, that a new kind of rhetoric was emerging which concealed its real essence, its basic character. It would be difficult for me to reconstruct those discussions exactly; all I remember is our ceaseless polemic against all the romanticized images, our reduction of the partisan consciousness to an elementary instinct, which we had observed even in the most unsophisticated of our comrades, and which became the key to the history of the present and the future.

My friend was very analytical in his arguments, cold and sarcastic about everything that was not an established fact; the only intellectual character in this novel, the commissar Kim, was intended to be a portrait of my friend; and something of our discussions in those days, particularly in the debate about why men who had no uniform or flag actually fought, must have survived in what I wrote, in Kim's dialogue with the brigade commandant and in his soliloquies.

These discussions were the background to the novel, and even further back were all my own thoughts on violence, from the minute I had found myself armed. Before joining the partisans, I had been a young middle-class boy who had always lived with his parents; my armchair anti-fascism had consisted primarily in a rejection of its cult of military force, and was more a question of style, of my particular 'sense of humour'; but suddenly to be consistent with these opinions meant I was thrust into the midst of partisan violence, and I had to measure myself on that scale. This was a real trauma for me, the first of many . . .

At the same time another element of the background to the book was a series of reflections on the moral judgments we should make about people and on the historical importance of the actions of each one of us. For many of my contemporaries it had been solely a question of luck which determined what side they should fight on; for many of them the sides suddenly changed over, so that soldiers of Mussolini's Fascist Republic became partisans and vice versa; they shot or were shot at on either side; only death signalled an end to their choices. (It was Pavese, caught between remorse for not having fought and the urge to be sincere about the reasons for his refusal, who managed to write, in the closing pages of *La casa in collina (The House on the Hill)*: 'Every casualty resembles the survivor and demands to know the reason for his death from those who survive.')

That's it now: I know how I should set out this preface. For months after the end of the war I had tried recounting the partisan experience in the first person, or with a protagonist very similar to myself. Some short stories I had published, others I put in the bin; I was uncomfortable with this material; I never managed to stifle entirely the moral and emotional feelings it aroused in me; something that rang false always emerged sooner or later; my own personal experience seemed banal and petty; I was a mass of complexes and inhibitions when confronted with all that I most dearly wanted to say.

But when I started writing stories in which I played no part, then everything began to click: the language, the narrative rhythm, the edge were all exactly right, and functioned well; the more objective and anonymous I made the story the more satisfied I was with it. Not only was I more satisfied, but also the people who were experts and whom I had come to know in those early post-war years – Vittorini and Giansiro Ferrata in Milan, Natalia Ginzburg and Pavese in Turin – they now no longer found anything to criticize. I began to realize that the more a story was objective and anonymous, the more it was my own.

This facility for writing 'objectively' seemed to me the most natural thing in the world; I could never have imagined that I would lose it so quickly. Each story moved perfectly naturally in a world which I knew intimately: that was *my* experience, my experience multiplied by the experience of the others. And the sense of history, the moral edge, the emotional element, were present precisely because I left them implicit and hidden.

When I began to expand a story about a little boy partisan whom I had known in the partisan groups, I did not think that it would become more substantial than the other stories. Why did it turn into a novel? Because – I later realized – the identification between myself and the protagonist had developed into something more complex. The relationship between the character of the boy Pin and the partisan war corresponded symbolically with the relationship that I myself had eventually had with that war. Pin's inferiority as a child facing the incomprehensible world of adults was the equivalent of the inferiority that I too felt in the same situation because of my middle-class upbringing. And Pin's uninhibited nature, stemming from his origins in the world of petty crime – about which he boasts so much – and which makes him feel on a par with other outlaws and almost superior to them, corresponded to the 'intellectual''s way of coping coolly with any situation, of never showing surprise, of keeping emotions at bay . . . So, interpreted in this key of symbolic substitutions – though I should make it clear that this was only an interpretation a posteriori, something which helped me subsequently understand what I had written – this story from which my own personal viewpoint had been banished, somehow came back to being *my own* story . . .

My own story was that of someone whose adolescence had gone on too long, a young man who had seized on the war as an *alibi*, both in the literal sense of going somewhere else, and in its metaphorical sense. In the space of just a few years the *alibi* had become the *here and now*. It was too soon for me; or too late: I was too unprepared to live out the dreams I had dreamed for too long. First came the reversal of the war against the Allies, the transformation of those who had previously been shadowy and subversive figures into heroes and leaders. Then in peace time new energies bubbled up which galvanized relationships and pervaded all the organs of public life, and suddenly even the distant castle of literature opened its gates like a safe and nearby haven, ready to welcome with flags and fanfares the young man from the provinces. And there was also an erotic charge which electrified the air and brightened the eyes of the girls whom the war and the peace had restored and brought closer to us: they were now truly of an age with us, our comrades, in a new rapport which was the fresh gift of those early months of peace, and which filled the warm evenings with conversation and laughter in an Italy reborn.

But in the face of all these possibilities which opened up for me, I never managed to become what I had dreamed I would be before I was put to the test: I had been the most insignificant of partisans; I was an uncertain, unsatisfied and inept lover; the world of literature did not open up for me like a straightforward and objective apprenticeship, but was more like a journey which I did not know how to start. Full of these youthful ambitions and anxieties, I lacked the spontaneous grace of youth. The rapid maturing of the times I lived in had only served to accentuate my own immaturity.

The symbolic protagonist of my novel was therefore an image of regression: a child. To the childish and jealous eyes of Pin, weapons and women seemed distant and incomprehensible; similarly what my philosophy wanted to exalt, my poetics transformed into hostile images, and my excessive love tinged with infernal despair.

When writing the book, my stylistic need was to write at a level below the events narrated: the kind of Italian I liked was that spoken by someone who 'doesn't speak proper Italian at home': I tried to write the way a hypothetical autodidact version of myself would have written.

The Path to the Spiders' Nests was born of this sense of total alienation, half suffered by me as a genuine torment, half imagined and vaunted. If I recognize any value in the book now it is in this: the image of a vital, but as yet hidden, strength in which the inadequacy felt by someone who was 'too young' bonded with the deprivations of society's exiles and rejects.

If I say that in those days we made literature out of our condition of poverty, I am not really talking about some ideological programme, but rather about something far more profound that was inside all of us.

Nowadays writing is a regularized profession and the novel is a 'product', with its own 'market', its own 'supply' and 'demand', with its launch campaigns, its successes and bouts of routine, and Italian novels are now all 'of good average quality' and form part of the surplus goods of a society which is all too easily satisfied. This makes it difficult to keep in mind the spirit which animated our attempts to establish a new tradition of fiction which had to be built entirely from scratch.

I am continuing to use the plural, but I have already explained that I am talking about something that was dispersed, not agreed upon, that emerged from remote corners of very different provinces, without any explicitly stated common motives other than those that were partial and temporary. More than anything else it was, so to speak, a potential that was in the air. A potential that was quickly exhausted.

By the 1950s the picture had already altered, starting with the major writers: Pavese was dead, Vittorini had retreated into an antagonistic silence, Moravia working in a different context was acquiring a different meaning (no longer an existentialist,

26

but rather a naturalist), and the Italian novel followed its course of moderate, elegiac, sociological analysis, in which we all in the end managed to carve ourselves a more or less comfortable niche (or found our escape route).

However, there were some who continued along the road of those early fragmentary epics: in general it was the most isolated writers, those who were least felt to 'belong', who retained that strength. And it was the most isolated of all of us who managed to write the novel that we had all dreamed of, when no one expected it any more, Beppe Fenoglio. He managed to write *Una questione privata (A Private Matter)* but not complete it, and he died in his mid-forties before seeing it published. The book that all our generation wanted to write now exists: our work has finally reached fulfilment and been given a sense of purpose, and only now, thanks to Fenoglio, can we say that a cycle is complete, only now can we be certain that such a cycle really existed, the cycle that goes from *The Path to the Spiders' Nests* to *Una questione privata*.

Una questione privata (which is now available in the post-humous volume *Un giorno di fuoco (A Day of Gunfire)*) is constructed with the kind of geometric tension found in romance epics about mad passions and knightly pursuits, such as Ariosto's *Orlando furioso*; yet at the same time it is about the Resistance exactly as it was, inside and out, a more authentic portrayal of the Resistance than has ever been in print, preserved with great clarity over many years by a faithful memory, and retaining all its moral values (which are all the stronger for being understated), as well as all its emotions and frenzies. It is also a book of landscapes, of rapidly sketched but vibrant figures, a book of words both precise and true. It is also an absurd, mysterious book, in which the object of pursuit is only pursued in order to pursue something else, and this

27

something else is in turn pursued for the sake of something else again, and we never reach the ultimate goal. It was the preface to Fenoglio's book, not to my own that I really wanted to write.

This is the first novel I wrote, almost my very first piece of writing. What can I say about it today? I will say this: it would be better never to have written your first novel.

Before you write your first book, you possess that freedom to begin writing that can be used only once in your life. The first book already defines you while you are in fact still far from being defined. And after that you have to carry this definition around with you for the rest of your life, trying to confirm it or develop it or modify it or even deny it, but no longer ever able to be without it.

There is another point: for those who start writing after one of those experiences that leave you with 'so many things to say' (the war in this, and in so many other cases), the first book instantly becomes a barrier between you and that experience, it severs the links that bind you to those facts, destroys your precious hoard of memories – a hoard in the sense that it would have become a reserve on which to draw permanently if you had been patient enough to husband it, if you had not been in such a hurry to spend it, to squander it, to impose an arbitrary hierarchy on the images that you had kept stored there, to separate the privileged images, which you believed contained a genuinely poetic emotion, from the others, those which seemed to concern you too closely or too little for you to be able to portray them; in short to set up in your arrogance a different memory, one that has been given another shape instead of your whole memory with its blurred outlines and its infinite capacity for retrieval . . . Your memory will never again recover from this violence that you have done to it by writing your book.

28

The privileged images will be spent because of their premature promotion to the level of literary themes, while the images that you wanted to keep in reserve, possibly with the intention of drawing on them in future works, will wither away because they are cut off from the organic wholeness of your fluid living memory. The habit of projecting things on to a literary plane where everything is solid and fixed once and for all, has now taken root, and has faded and crushed the crop of memories in which the life of the tree and of the blade of grass mutually nourish each other. Memory, or rather experience – which is the memory of the event plus the wound it has inflicted on you, plus the change which it has wrought in you and which has made you different – experience is the basic nutrition also for a work of literature (but not only for that), the true source of wealth for every writer (but not only for the writer), and yet the minute it gives shape to a work of literature it withers and dies. The writer, after writing, finds that he is the poorest of men.

This is, then, how I look back at that period which seemed at the time to be burgeoning with images and meanings: the partisan war, the months which had counted for years in my life, and from which one ought to be able indefinitely to conjure up faces and messages and landscapes and thoughts and episodes and words and emotions. But everything is distant and misty, while the pages stand there in their impudent permanence which I know to be deceptive, pages which even then were at variance with a memory which was still a living presence, something solid, apparently stable and permanent, an *experience* – and those pages are no use to me, I really would need all the other things, everything in fact that is not written down in those pages. A completed book will never compensate me for what I destroyed in writing it: namely that experience which if preserved throughout the years of my life might have helped to compose my last book, and which in fact was sufficient only to write the first.

I.C.
June 1964

CHAPTER ONE

To reach the depths of the alley, the sun's rays have to plunge down vertically, grazing the cold walls which are kept apart by stone arches spanning the strip of deep blue sky.

Down they plunge, the sun's rays, past windows dotted at random over the walls, and plants of basil and oregano in cooking-pots on the sills, and underwear hung out to dry; right down they go until they reach the cobbled, stepped alleyway with its gutter in the middle for the mules' urine.

Pin, standing on the doorstep of the cobbler's shop, with his nose in the air, just has to give a cry from his throat – a cry to start off a song, or a yell just before the hand of Pietromagro the cobbler lands on the back of his neck to strike him – and a chorus of shouts and insults pours from every window.

'Pin! At it already, making our lives a misery! Sing us one of your songs, Pin! Pin, you little hooligan, what's he doing to you? Pin, you little monkey-face! Why don't you just wrap up? You and that chicken-thief of a master of yours! You and that mattress of a sister of yours!'

But by now, Pin is standing in the middle of the alley, with his hands in the pockets of a jacket that is too big for him, looking up at them one by one with an unsmiling face: 'Hey, Celestino, you'd better keep quiet, wearing that fine new suit. They haven't found out yet who stole that stuff from the New Harbour, have they? Of course, there's no connection between the two.

Oh hi, Carolina, you were lucky that time. Yes. Lucky your husband didn't look under the bed, remember? You as well, Pasquale. They told me what actually happened in your village: you know, that when Garibaldi finally brought you soap your fellow-villagers thought it was for eating. Soapeaters, Pasquale! For God's sake, have you any idea how much soap costs?'

Pin has the hoarse voice of a much older boy; he shouts out his jeers in deep, serious tones, then suddenly breaks into a laugh with a note as high and sharp as a whistle, while ginger and brown freckles cluster up round his eyes like a swarm of wasps.

Insulting Pin is always risky; he knows all the inside gossip of the alley and one can never tell what he'll come out with. From morning till night he's out there under the windows singing and shouting at the top of his voice, while in Pietromagro's shop the pile of unmended shoes almost buries the cobbler's bench and spills out into the street.

'Pin, you little monkey! You little horror!' a woman shouts at him. 'Resole those slippers for me instead of standing there making a nuisance of yourself all day! They've been in that pile a month. I'll have something to say to your boss when they let him out!'

Pietromagro spends half his life in prison, for he was born unlucky, and whenever there's a theft in the neighbourhood he's always the one to be put inside eventually. He gets out to find that great pile of unmended shoes in an empty shop. Then he sits down at his cobbler's bench, takes up a shoe, turns it over once or twice, throws it back into the heap, and finally puts his hairy face into his bony hands and begins swearing. When Pin, completely unaware, comes in whistling, he is suddenly confronted by Pietromagro, with a face covered in short black hair like dog's fur, eyes ringed with yellow round the pupils, and hand upraised. Pin screams, but Pietromagro has already caught him and does not let go. When Pietromagro is tired of hitting Pin he leaves him in the shop and makes for the tavern. No one sees any more of him that day.

On alternate evenings, Pin's sister is visited by a German sailor. Every time the man makes his way up the alley, Pin waits for him to ask for a cigarette. The sailor was generous at first and even gave him three or four at a time. It's easy for Pin to make fun of the German, who can't understand what he says and looks at him from a shapeless congealed-looking face, shaven to the temples. Then, when the sailor's back is turned, Pin can shout insults after him, certain he won't turn round. Seen from behind the sailor looks ridiculous, with those two black ribbons hanging down from his little cap over his short tunic to his bare-looking bottom; a fleshy bottom, like a woman's, with a big German pistol dangling over it.

'You little pimp . . . little pimp . . .' people call down from the windows at Pin, not too loudly though, as one never knows with those Germans.

'I may be a pimp, but I know what your wives are up to behind your backs . . .' Pin shouts back, copying their voices, and gulping down cigarette smoke that feels sharp and rough against his tender throat, but which has to be gulped down, who knows why, till his eyes water and he breaks into a violent fit of coughing. Then, with the cigarette still in his mouth, off he goes to the tavern and calls out: 'By God, I'll tell anyone who stands me a glass of wine something he'd like to hear.'

In the tavern are the same men who have been there all day long for years, sitting with their elbows on the tables and their chins in their fists, gazing at the flies on the sticky paper and the purple stains in the bottom of their glasses.

'What's up?' says Michel the Frenchman. 'Your sister drop-ped her prices, has she?'

The others laugh and pound their fists on the zinc table-tops: 'You asked for that one, Pin!'

Pin stands there looking them up and down through the spiky fringe of hair standing up on his forehead.

'God, just as I thought. Look at him, he thinks of nothing but my sister. Never stops thinking of her, I tell you. He's in love. In love with my sister, God help him . . .'

The others roar with laughter and clap him on the back and pour him out a glass. Pin does not like wine; it feels harsh against his throat and gives him goose-flesh and makes him long to laugh and shout and stir up trouble. Yet he drinks it, swallowing down each glassful in one gulp, as he swallows cigarette smoke, or as at night he watches with shivers of disgust his sister lying with some man on her bed, a sight like the feel of a rough caress against his skin, harsh like all sensations men enjoy; smoke, wine, women.

'Sing, Pin,' they say. And Pin begins singing, seriously, tensely, in that hoarse childish voice of his. He sings a song called 'The Four Seasons':

> *When I think of the future*
> *And the liberty I've lost*
> *I'd like to kiss her and then die*
> *While she sleeps . . . and never knows.*

The men sit in silence, with their eyes lowered, as if listening to a hymn. All of them have been in prison; no one is a real man to them unless he has. And the old jail-birds' song is full of the melancholy which seeps into the bones in prison, at night, when the warders pass hitting the grills with a crowbar, and gradually the quarrels and curses die down, and all that can still be heard is a voice singing this song which Pin is singing now, and which no one shouts for him to stop.

> At night I love to hear
> The sentry's call,
> I love to watch the passing moon
> Light up my cell.

Pin has never been in a real prison yet; once when they tried to take him off to a reformatory he escaped. Every now and again he is picked up by the municipal guards for some escapade among the stalls in the fruit-market, but he always sends the guards nearly crazy with his screams and sobs, until finally they let him go. He has been shut up in their guardroom once or twice, though, and knows what prison feels like; that's why he is singing this song so well, with real emotion.

Pin knows all those old songs which have been taught him by the men of the tavern, songs about violence and bloodshed such as 'Torna Caserio' or the one about a soldier called Peppino who killed his lieutenant. Then, when they are all feeling sad and gazing into the purple depths of their glasses, Pin suddenly twirls round the smoky room and begins singing at the top of his voice:

> And I touched her hair –
> And she said not there
> Go down where there's nicer hair:
> Darling, if you love me,
> Touch me lower down . . .

Then the men begin pounding on the tables and shouting 'hiuú,' and clapping time, while the serving-girl tries to save the glasses. And the women in the tavern, old drunks with red faces like the one called the Bersagliera, sway to and fro as if

35

to the rhythm of a dance. And Pin, his blood up, grits his teeth with the effort, and seems to be throwing his very soul into the song as he shouts at the top of his voice:

> *And I touched her little nose –*
> *And she said, that's a foolish pose*
> *Go down to my garden rose . . .*

And all of them, clapping time to the swaying of the old Bersagliera, break into the chorus: 'Darling, *if you love me . . .*'

That day the German sailor had come up the alley in a bad temper. Hamburg, his native town, was being ravaged by bombs every night, and every day he was waiting for news of his wife and children. He had a warm nature, this German had, a southern nature in the body of a man from the North Sea. He had filled his own home with children, and now, when the war had moved him far away, tried to find some outlet for his feelings of human affection by befriending prostitutes in the occupied countries.

'No cigarettes,' he had said to Pin who was coming towards him to say *guten Tag*. Pin began to frown at him.

'Well, *Kamerad*, back again today? You're getting homesick for this place, eh?' he said.

Now it was the German's turn to frown at Pin; he could not understand.

'Are you on your way to visit my sister, by any chance?' said Pin innocently.

The German then said: 'Sister not home?'

'What, haven't you heard?' Pin's expression was so sly he might have been brought up by priests. 'Don't you know they've taken her off to hospital? Poor thing! It's bad, that disease, but curable now, if it's treated in time. Of course she'd had it on her for a bit . . . think of her in hospital, poor thing!'

The German's face looked like curdled milk. 'Hos-pit-al? Di-sea-se?' he stuttered and sweated. Then in a window just above the ground floor appeared the head and shoulders of a young woman with a horse face and frizzy black hair.

'Don't you take any notice of him, Frick, don't take any notice of the little squirt,' she screamed. 'I'll make you pay for this, monkey-face, you nearly ruined me! Come on up, Frick, don't take any notice of him, he was only joking, devil take him!'

Pin put his tongue out at her. 'I got you into a cold sweat, *Kamerad*,' he said to the German, as he slipped away down a side-alley.

Sometimes, after a malicious joke of that kind, Pin finds himself with a bitter taste in his mouth, and wanders round the alleys alone, with everyone cursing him and pushing him aside. Then he longs to go off with a band of young companions to whom he could show the place where spiders make their nests, or with whom he could have battles among the bamboos in the river-bed. But Pin is not liked by boys of his own age; he is the friend of grown-ups, Pin is, he can say things to grown-ups that make them laugh or get angry, while other boys can't even understand what grown-ups say to each other. Pin sometimes feels a longing to join boys of his own age and to ask them to let him play with them, to show him the way into the underground passage that goes right under the Market Square. But the other boys leave him out of their games; sometimes they even set on him, for Pin has tiny thin arms and is the weakest of them all. Now and again they go and ask Pin to explain what happens between men and women; but he begins making fun of them in a loud voice down the alley, and the mothers call their sons inside: 'Costanzo! Giacomino! How often have I told you not to go about with that nasty little boy!'

The mothers are right. All Pin talks about is men and women

in bed, or men murdered or put in prison, stories picked up from grown-ups, fables they tell among themselves – the other little boys think – and which would be nice to stop and listen to if only Pin did not intersperse them with jeers and remarks they cannot understand.

So Pin is forced to take refuge again in the world of grown-ups, of men who turn their backs on him and are as incomprehensible and far-removed from him as they are from the other little boys, but who are easier to make fun of, with their yearning for women and their terror of the police, till they tire of him and begin to clip him round the ear.

Now Pin will go back into the smoky violet air of the tavern, and mouth obscenities and insults to the men there until he has whipped them up into a frenzy and they begin attacking each other; then he'll sing sentimental songs with all his might till he makes them cry and is crying himself, then invent new jokes and grimaces till he's hysterical with laughter, all to disperse the cloud of loneliness which settles round his heart on evenings like this.

But the men in the tavern now all have their backs turned, forming an impenetrable wall; there in the middle of them is a newcomer, a thin serious-looking man. As Pin comes in the men frown at him, then at the unknown man, and say something. Pin feels that the atmosphere is different; all the more reason to go up to the group with his hands in his pockets and say: 'God, you ought to have seen that German's face!'

The men don't make their usual joking replies, but turn slowly round one by one. Michel the Frenchman first frowns at him as if he's never seen him before, then says slowly: 'You're a filthy little pimp.'

The freckles cloud up like wasps round Pin's eyes, then he says calmly, though his eyes are slits: 'Perhaps you'll tell me why?'

Giraffe twists his neck slightly round towards him and says: 'Off you go, we don't want to see anyone who deals with Germans.'

'With your contacts, you and your sister,' says Gian the driver, 'you'll end up as Fascist big shots.'

Pin tries to put on the expression he uses when making fun of them.

'Perhaps you'll tell me what all this is about,' he says, 'I've never had anything to do with the Fascio, not even the Balilla, and my sister goes with whoever she wants and does no one any harm.'

Michel scratches his face a little. 'The day everything changes – you know what I mean – the day everything changes we'll send your sister round town with her head as shaved and bare as a plucked chicken . . . And for you . . . for you we'll think up something you haven't even dreamt of.'

Pin does his best to look unconcerned, but is obviously suffering inwardly, and is biting his lips. 'On the day when you get a bit brighter,' he says, 'I'll explain how things are. First, that I and my sister each go our own way, and as for pimping you can go and do it for her yourself if you feel like it. Second, that my sister doesn't go with Germans because she particularly likes them, but because she's as international as the Red Cross; and the same way she goes with Germans now she'll go later with English, Negroes and anyone else who happens to turn up' . . . (all these are things Pin has learnt from listening to grown-ups, probably the very same ones talking to him now. Why should he have to explain them?) 'Third, the only dealings I've had with that German is getting cigarettes out of him, in return for which I've played tricks on him like the one I did today, which I won't tell you about now as you've put me in a bad temper.'

But the attempt to change the subject does not succeed. Gian

39

the driver says: 'Tricks! I've been in Croatia and there a bloody German only had to go looking round a village for women, and he was never seen again, nor was his corpse.'

Michel says: 'One day or the other he'll be found dead in the sewers, your German will.'

The unknown man, who has been silent all this time without smiling or showing any signs of approval, now pulls Michel by the sleeve a little: 'That's the sort of thing you mustn't say. Remember what I told you.'

The others nod and are still looking at Pin in silence. What can they want of him?

'Listen,' exclaims Michel, 'have you seen what a pistol that sailor has?'

'Yes, a hell of a big pistol,' replies Pin.

'Well,' says Michel, 'you must bring us that pistol.'

'How can I do that?' exclaims Pin.

'Try.'

'But how? He always wears it clamped to his bottom. You go and steal it.'

'Well, let's see . . . He's got to take his trousers off at some stage, doesn't he? Then he must take his pistol off too, surely. Go and steal it. Try.'

'I will if I feel like it.'

'Listen,' says Giraffe, 'we aren't joking here. If you want to be one of us you now know what you must do. Otherwise . . .'

'Otherwise . . .'

'Otherwise . . . D'you know what a G.A.P.[1] is?'

The unknown man gives Giraffe a nudge and shakes his head; he does not seem to like the way the others are behaving.

New words to Pin always have a halo of mystery, a hint

---

[1] *Gruppo Azione Patrioti.* The smallest unit of the Italian partisan organization, usually in towns.

of something dark and forbidden. A *Gap*? What could a *Gap* be?

'Yes, of course I know what it is,' he says.

'What is it?' asks Giraffe.

'It's where you all blasted well belong, you and your family.'

But the men aren't listening to him. The unknown man has signalled to them to bring their heads closer and is whispering to them and seems to be rebuking them for something, and they are making signs of agreement.

Pin is out of all this. He can creep away without saying a word; perhaps it's best, he thinks, not to mention that business of the pistol any more, it probably wasn't important, and they may have forgotten all about it.

But Pin has just reached the door when Michel raises his head and says: 'Pin, then we're agreed about that.'

Pin would like to begin acting the fool again, but suddenly he feels a child surrounded by grown-ups, and stands there with his hand on the jamb of the door.

'If not, don't put your face in here again,' says Michel.

Now Pin is outside, in the alley. Dusk is falling and lights are going on in the windows. Far away, down by the river, frogs are beginning to croak; at this time of the year boys spend their evenings hanging over pools, trying to catch them. When caught, the frogs feel slimy and slithery in their hands, smooth and naked as women.

A little boy in glasses and long trousers passes by: Battistino.

'Battistino, d'you know what a *Gap* is?'

Battistino blinks with curiosity. 'No, tell me. What is it?'

Pin breaks out into a peal of laughter. 'Just go and ask your mother what a *Gap* is. Say to her, "Mummy, will you give me a *Gap*?" Say that. She'll explain, you'll see!'

Battistino slopes off, looking humiliated.

41

Pin wanders up the alley, which is almost dark now, and feels alone and lost amid all this talk of bloodshed and naked bodies which makes up men's lives.

CHAPTER TWO

His sister's room, from where Pin is looking at it, seems filled with mist; he can see a vertical strip crowded with objects and surrounded by muzzy shadows, with everything changing dimensions according to whether he puts his eye nearer or farther from the slit. It's like looking through a woman's stocking; the smell is the same too: his sister's smell emanating from the other side of the wooden partition and coming perhaps from those rumpled clothes and that bed which is never properly made, the sheets just flung back without ever being aired.

Pin's sister has always been careless about household matters ever since she was a child; when Pin was a baby and used to cry loudly in her arms, his head covered in scabs, she would leave him on a ledge of the wash-house and go off to skip with urchins around the chalk squares marked on the pavements. Every now and again their father's ship would return; all Pin could remember of him was being swung in the air in his big, bare arms, strong arms marked with black veins. But after their mother's death his visits became rarer and rarer, until he was never seen again; people said he had another family in a city beyond the sea.

Pin now lives in a cubby-hole of a room, a sort of kennel beyond a wooden partition, with a high narrow slit of a window, cut sideways through the thick wall of the old house.

Beyond it is his sister's room, which he can see filtered through the cracks in the partition, cracks which make Pin's eyes squint with the effort to see what's going on in the rest of the room. The meaning of everything in the world is supplied by what goes on beyond that partition; Pin has spent hours and hours at those cracks ever since he was a baby, and he's trained his eyes to be like needle points; he knows everything that happens inside there, though the reasons for it all elude him. When, in the end, he curls up in his little bunk with his arms round his chest, the shadows of the tiny room transform themselves into strange dreams, of naked bodies chasing, hitting and embracing each other, till something big and hot and unknown comes and hovers over Pin and yet caresses and warms him too; and this is the explanation of everything, like the faint distant memory of some forgotten happiness.

The German is now wandering round the room in his vest, his arms pink and meaty as thighs; every now and again he comes into focus at the crack in the partition; at one moment Pin can also see his sister's legs, twirling in the air, then plunging under the sheets. Now Pin has to twist round to see where the German is putting down the belt with the pistol on it; there it is, hung on the back of a chair like some strange fruit; Pin wishes he had an arm as narrow as the slit so that he could slip it through, reach the weapon and pull it towards him. Now the German is naked except for his vest; he's laughing; he always laughs when he's naked because he is shy, deep down, like a girl. He jumps into bed and puts out the light. Pin knows that a little time will go by in darkness and silence before the bed begins to creak.

Now is the moment. Pin must enter the room with bare feet, on all fours, and pull the belt down from the chair without making any noise; all this is not just a game to laugh and joke about afterwards; no, it is connected with something secret and mysterious said by the men in the tavern with an opaque

43

look in the whites of their eyes. Yet, Pin would like always to be friends with grown-ups, for them always to joke with him and to take him into their confidence. Pin loves grown-ups, he loves winding them up – those strong stupid grown-ups all of whose secrets he knows. He even loves the German. And now he is doing something irrevocable; perhaps he'll never be able to joke with the German again, after this; and things will be different with the men in the tavern, too; they'll have a link with him beyond laughter and obscenities, and will always look at him with those mysterious frowns and ask him stranger and stranger things in low voices. Pin would like to stretch himself out on his little bed and lie there thinking with his eyes open, listening to the German panting and his sister moaning on the other side of the partition, lie there imagining himself being accepted by bands of boys as their leader because he knows so much more than they do, and them all going out against the grown-ups together and beating them up and doing such wonderful things that the grown-ups are forced to admire him too and ask him to be their leader, loving him and stroking his head at the same time. But now, instead of that, he has to move about at night all on his own, with the grown-ups hating him, and steal a pistol from a German, things not done by other boys, who play with tin pistols and wooden swords. What would they say if Pin went among them next day, and gradually revealed to them a real pistol, all shiny and menacing and looking as if it were about to go off on its own? Perhaps they would be frightened, and Pin would also be frightened of keeping such a thing under his jacket; all he needs, he thinks, to terrify the grown-ups so much that they fall down fainting and asking for mercy, is one of those toy pistols that fire a strip of red caps.

Instead of which Pin is now crawling on all fours into his sister's room, bare foot, with his head already beyond the curtain, into that smell of male and female which goes straight to the nostrils. He can see the shadows of the furniture in the room, the bed, the chair, the oblong bidet on its triangular stand. There; now that dialogue of groans is beginning from the bed, and he can creep ahead on all fours, taking care to go very slowly. Perhaps, though, Pin would prefer if the floor creaked, the German heard and suddenly put on the light, and he had to run out of the house on bare feet with his sister shouting behind him: 'Little swine!'; prefer it, perhaps, if the whole neighbourhood heard too and people talked of it in the tavern as well, and he could tell the story to Driver and the Frenchman, with so many details that they would believe him and say: 'All right. It didn't come off. Don't let's talk about it any more.'

The floor does in fact creak, but so many other things are creaking at that moment that the German does not hear. Pin is now touching the belt, and it turns out to be quite solid, not magical, and it slips down from the back of the chair almost frighteningly easily, without even banging on the floor. Now 'it' has happened; the fear he had only imagined before has become real fear. The belt must now be hurriedly wrapped round the holster, and all of it pushed under his jumper without getting entangled in his arms and legs; the next thing to do is go back on his tracks on all fours, very slowly and without ever taking his tongue from between his teeth; if he took that tongue away perhaps something awful would happen.

Once out of the room, he realizes that he can't now go back to his little bed and hide the pistol under the mattress, as he does with apples stolen from the fruit market. In a short time the German will be getting up and looking for his pistol and turning the whole place upside down.

Pin goes out into the alley; the pistol is not worrying him very much at the moment; hidden like that in his clothes it is an object like any other and he can forget he has it; Pin rather regrets his own indifference, and would like to feel at least a shiver whenever he thinks about it. A real pistol. A real pistol. Pin tries to excite himself with the thought. Someone who has a real pistol can do anything, he's like a grown-up. He can threaten to kill men and women and do whatever he likes with them.

Pin now thinks he will grasp the pistol and walk round with it always pointed at people; no one will be able to take it away from him and everyone will be afraid of him. But the pistol, wrapped in its belt, is still under his jumper, and he cannot make up his mind to touch it; in a way he almost hopes that when he looks for it, it will have vanished, melted away by the heat of his body.

The place to look at the pistol is a hidden flight of steps under an arch where children go to play hide-and-seek, lit only by a glimmer of light from a twisted street lamp. Pin unrolls the belt, opens the holster, and with a gesture as if he were taking a cat by the neck pulls out the pistol. It is really very big and threatening; if Pin had the courage to play with it he would pretend it was a cannon. But he handles it as if it were a bomb. The safety-catch, where can the safety-catch be?

Finally he decides to grasp it by the butt, though he's careful not to put his finger near the trigger; he holds it tightly; even like this he can still hold it properly and point it against anyone he wants. Pin first points it at the gutter-pipe, right up against the metal, then at a finger, one of his own fingers, making a fierce face, drawing back his head and hissing: 'Your money or your life'; then he finds an old shoe and points it against that, first the heel, then the inside; then he runs the barrel along the stitching of the uppers. What fun! A shoe, such an ordinary object, particularly for a cobbler's apprentice like him, and a pistol, such a mysterious, almost unreal thing; by putting them up against each other he can do wonders, make them tell marvellous tales.

But then suddenly Pin cannot resist the temptation any more and points the pistol against his temple; it makes his head swim. On it moves, until it touches the skin and he can feel the coldness of the steel. Suppose he put his finger on the trigger now? No, it's better to press the mouth of the barrel against the top of his cheek bone, until it hurts, and feel the circle of steel with its empty centre where the bullets come from. Perhaps if he suddenly pulls the gun away from his temple, the suction of the air will make a shot go off; no, it doesn't go off. Now he can put the barrel into his mouth and feel its taste against his tongue. Then, the most frightening of all, put it up to his eyes and look right into it, down the dark barrel which seems deep as a well. Once Pin saw a boy who had shot himself in the eye with a hunting-gun being taken off to hospital; his face was half-covered by a great splodge of blood, and the other half with little black spots from the gunpowder.

Pin has now played with a real pistol. He has played with it enough, and can give it to the men who asked for it, he now can't wait to give it to them, in fact. When he has not got it any more it will be the same as if he'd never stolen it, and the German can be as furious as he likes and Pin can laugh at him behind his back again.

His first impulse is to rush into the tavern and call out: 'I've got it! I've got it!' amid general enthusiasm and exclamations of surprise. Then it occurs to him that it would be cleverer to say: 'Guess what I've brought!' and keep them waiting a little before telling them. But they would be sure to think of the pistol at once, so he had better mention it at first and then go on to give them a dozen different versions of what happened, hinting that things went badly, until when they are on tenterhooks and have lost the drift, he'd put the pistol on the table and say: 'Look what I've found in my pocket,' and watch the expressions on their faces.

Pin enters the tavern silently, on tiptoe; the men are still talking round a table, their elbows rigid as if they had taken root. Only the unknown man is no longer there; his chair is empty. Pin is now standing behind them and they have not noticed him; he waits for them to catch sight of him suddenly and start up with questioning looks. But no one turns. Pin moves a chair. Giraffe twists his neck round and frowns at him, then goes on talking in a low voice.

'Hey, guys,' exclaims Pin.

They give him a glance.

'Uglyface,' says Giraffe, in a friendly way.

No one says anything else.

'Well . . .' says Pin.

'Well . . .' says Gian the driver. 'What's new?'

Pin is beginning to feel rather deflated.

'Well . . .' says Michel the Frenchman. 'Feeling low? Sing us a song, Pin.'

They're pretending not to be interested, thinks Pin, but really they're dying to know what I've done.

'Right then,' says Pin. But this doesn't work: his throat is dry, it feels as if he has a lump in it like when he is afraid of breaking down and crying.

'Right then,' he says again. 'Which song do you want?'

'Which song?' echoes Michel.

Giraffe then says, 'How boring it is tonight, I wish I was home in my bed.'

Pin is now fed up with this game and asks, 'And what about that man?'

'Who?'

'The man who was sitting there before?'

'Ah,' the others reply, shaking their heads. Then they start talking in a low voice again.

'I for one,' says Michel to the others, 'would not want to compromise myself too much for these people from the Committee. I don't feel like risking my skin just to save their faces.'

'It's alright,' says Gian the driver. 'After all, what have we agreed to? We said we'll see. For the time being it is in our interests to have some connection with them without committing ourselves, and to bide our time. In my case I've got a score to settle with the Germans from the time I served on the front with them, and if it's a case of getting stuck in, I'm willing enough.'

'That's all very well,' says Michel, 'but remember that the Germans are no laughing matter, and no one knows how all this is going to end up. The Committee wants us to form a *Gap*; right then, we'll set up our own *Gap*.'

'Meanwhile,' says Giraffe, 'we'll show them that we're on their side and get guns. Once we've got guns, though . . .'

Pin has a gun: he can feel the pistol underneath his jacket, and puts his hand over it, as though the men were about to take it from him.

'Have you got arms?' he asks.

'Don't you worry about that,' exclaims Giraffe. 'You worry about getting hold of that German's pistol, as we'd agreed.'

Pin's ears go up. Now he'll say: 'Just guess . . .'

'Make sure you don't lose sight of it, once you've set eyes on it.'

This is not what Pin expected. Why are they so uninterested in it now? He begins to wish he had not taken the pistol, and feels like going back to the German and putting it back where it was.

'For one pistol,' says Michel. 'It's not worth the risk. Anyway it's an old model; heavy, it jams.'

'Still,' says Giraffe, 'we must show the committee we're doing something, that's the important thing.' And they continue their discussion in low voices.

Pin cannot hear what they are saying. Now he's sure he won't give them the pistol; he has tears in his eyes and can feel his gums drawn with rage. Grown-ups are an untrustworthy, treacherous lot, they don't take their games in the serious wholehearted way children do, and yet they too have their own games, one more serious than the other, one game inside another, so that it's impossible to discover what the real one is. Before it seemed that they were playing a game with the unknown man against the German, now they are playing one on their own against the unknown man; what they say can never be trusted.

'Well, sing us something, then, Pin,' they say now, as if nothing had happened, as if there had never been that definite pact between them, a pact consecrated by that mysterious word: *Gap*.

'*Alé*,' says Pin, pale, his lips trembling. He knows he cannot sing now. He feels like bursting into tears; instead of which he breaks into a shriek high enough to break the eardrums, ending in a string of curses: 'Bastards! The mother of every one of you was a pox-ridden bitch, a filthy stinking cow of a whore!'

The others stare at him, wondering what is wrong with him, but Pin has already rushed out of the tavern.

Outside, his first impulse is to look for that man, the one they call 'Committee', and give him the pistol; he's the only one for whom Pin feels any respect now, though he had been so quiet and serious he had made Pin distrustful before. But now Pin feels that he is the only person who can understand him and admire what he has done; perhaps 'Committee' would take Pin off to fight the Germans with him, just the two of them, armed with that pistol, firing from street corners. But who knew where Committee had gone to now? Pin cannot ask around after him, as no one had ever seen him before.

So Pin decides that he will keep the pistol himself and not give it to anyone or tell anyone that he has it. He'll just hint that he possesses a terrible power, and everyone will obey him. Whoever owns a real pistol must be able to play wonderful games, games which no other boy has ever played. But Pin is a boy who does not know how to play games, and cannot take part in the games either of children or grown-ups. So he will go off now, away from everyone, and play with his pistol all on his own, games that no one else knows and no one else can ever learn.

It is dark now. Pin turns out of the huddle of old houses into paths running between vegetable patches and rubbish-pits. The wire-netting around the crops throws a network of grey shadows over the moonlit ground. The hens are now sleeping in rows on their perches in the coops, and the frogs are out of the water and chorusing away along the bed of the whole torrent, from source to mouth. What would happen if he shot at a frog? There'd be nothing left, perhaps, but green slime squashed on the stones.

Pin wanders along the paths which wind along the side of the torrent, steep parts which no one cultivates. Here there are paths which he alone knows and which the other boys would love to be told about. There is a place where spiders make their nests. Only Pin knows it. He's the only one in the whole valley, perhaps in the whole area. No other boy except Pin has ever heard of spiders that make nests.

Perhaps one day Pin will find a friend, a real friend, who understands him and whom he can understand, and then to him, and only to him, will he show the place where the spiders have their lairs. It's on a stony little path which winds down to the torrent between earthy grassy slopes. There, in the grass, the spiders make their nests, in tunnels lined with dry grass. But the wonderful thing is that the nests have tiny doors, also made of dried grass, tiny round doors which can open and shut.

When Pin has played some particularly cruel joke and has laughed so much that a heavy sadness has finally filled his chest, he wanders all alone along the paths by the torrent, looking for the place where the spiders make their nests. With a long stick he can probe right into the nests and skewer the spider, a small black spider with little grey markings on it, like those on the summer dresses of old village women.

It amuses Pin to break the doors of the nests down and skewer the spiders on sticks, and to catch grasshoppers and gaze close into their absurd, green, horse-like faces, then cut them up into pieces and make strange designs with their legs on a smooth stone.

Pin is cruel to animals; to him they are as monstrous and incomprehensible as grown-ups; it must be horrible to be an insect, to be green and to shit in little drops, and always to be frightened that a human being like him might come along, with a huge face full of ginger and brown freckles, and fingers that can pull grasshoppers to bits.

Pin is now all alone among the spiders' nests, and around him is night, infinite as the chorus of the frogs. He is alone but he has the pistol with him; now he puts on the belt with its holster to dangle over his bottom like the German; only the German was so fat the belt was large enough to be worn round Pin's neck like the bandoliers worn by warriors in the films. Now he can pull the pistol out with a grand gesture as if he were drawing a sword, and shout: 'Forward, men!' as boys do when they play at pirates. But he cannot understand what pleasure those silly fools get in saying and doing that; Pin, after jumping around on the grass for a time, waving the pistol and aiming it at the shadows of olive trees, is already bored and does not know what to do with the gun next.

At that moment the spiders underground are gnawing away at worms or coupling together, males and females, giving out little threads of slime; they are as filthy as men are, Pin thinks, and he pushes the barrel of the pistol into the opening of a nest, longing to kill them. What would happen if a shot went off? The houses are some way off and no one would realize where it came from.

Pin now has his finger on the trigger, with the pistol pointed into a spider's nest; it is difficult to resist the longing to press the trigger, but the safety-catch must be on and he does not know how to cope with it.

Then a shot goes off so suddenly that Pin does not even realize he has fired it; the pistol jumps back in his hand, smoking and dirty all over with earth. The tunnel of the nest has collapsed; on to it has fallen a little landslide of earth and the grass is singed.

At first Pin is terrified, then delighted. How lovely it was, how good the powder smells! But then he is terrified again to find the frogs have suddenly all gone silent and not a sound is to be heard, as if that shot had killed off the entire world. Then, very far away, a frog begins to croak again, and another nearer by, and others nearer still, till the chorus starts up again and the croaking seems to Pin louder, much louder, than before. From the houses a dog barks and a woman calls from a window. Pin thinks he won't fire again, for that silence and then those sounds have frightened him. But he'll come back another night and nothing will frighten him then; he'll fire every round in the pistol, even at the bats and the cats prowling round the chicken-coops.

Now he must find a place to hide the pistol; in the trunk of an olive tree; or burying it would be better; or better still scoop out a hole in the grassy bank where the spiders' nests are and cover it over with mould and grass. Pin begins scooping away with his hands at a part where the earth is already honeycombed with tunnels made by the spiders, takes the pistol off its belt and puts it into the holster, and covers it all over with mould and grass and bits from the walls of chewed grass made by the spiders. Then he places some stones so that he can recognize the spot, and runs off lashing out at the bushes with the gun-belt. His way home takes him back along the little man-made channels running above the torrent-bed, with narrow lines of stones to walk on.

As he goes along Pin is dangling the end of the belt in the water and whistling so as not to hear the chorus of frogs which seems to be getting louder every moment.

Now he is among the little gardens and the rubbish dumps outside the houses. As he reaches them he hears voices, not talking in Italian. Pin often goes round at night in spite of the curfew and the patrols don't say anything to him because he's only a child. But this time he is afraid, as it occurs to him that those Germans there may be looking for the person who fired a gun. They come towards him and he tries to run away; but they shout something and catch him up. Pin takes up a position of defence, holding the belt as if it were a whip. But that is what the Germans are looking at, it's the belt they are after; and suddenly they take him by the scruff of the neck and drag him off. Pin talks ceaselessly; begs, complains, insults, but the Germans do not understand any of it; they are worse, much worse, than the municipal guards.

The alley is crowded with armed German and Fascist patrols, and men they have arrested, including Michel the Frenchman. Pin has to pass through these on his way up the alley. It is very dark; the only light comes from the top of the steps, from a lamp that only lets out a glimmer because of the black-out.

By the light of the glimmer, at the top of the alley, Pin sees the sailor, his fat face distorted with fury, pointing a finger at him.

CHAPTER THREE

Yes, the Germans are worse than the municipal guards. With the guards Pin could at least, if nothing else, begin joking, and say: 'If you let me go I'll arrange for you to go to bed free with my sister.'

But the Germans cannot even understand what he says, and the Fascists are men he has never seen before, men who do not even know who his sister is. Both are strange types; the Germans are as ruddy, fleshy, and hairless as the Fascists are black, bony, and bluish in the face, with rat-like moustaches.

Next morning, at the German headquarters, Pin is the first to be interrogated. He is faced by a German officer with a baby-like face, and a Fascist interpreter with a little beard. In a corner is the sailor, and, sitting near him, Pin's sister. They are all looking bored; the sailor seems to have made up a long story about the stolen pistol, so as not to get any blame for letting it be stolen, and must have told a lot of lies.

On the officer's table lies the belt, and the first question Pin is asked is: 'How did you get hold of this?' Pin is half asleep; he has spent the night on the floor in a passage with Michel the Frenchman near him and every time Pin was getting off to sleep Michel gave him a violent dig in the ribs with his elbow and whispered: 'If you talk I'll kill you.'

Pin had replied each time: 'Oh, piss off.'

Michel said: 'You mustn't say a word about us, d'you understand? Not even if they beat you.'

And Pin replied: 'Oh, go and shoot yourself.'

'We've all agreed that if the others don't see me come home they'll kill you.'

And Pin replied: 'I hope your soul rots in hell.'

Michel is one of those people who used to work in hotels in France before the war; he'd had quite a good time there on the whole, though sometimes they would call him *macaroni* or *cochon fasciste*, then in '40 he began being put into concentration camps and everything had gone wrong with him since: unemployment, repatriation, law-breaking.

Suddenly the sentries had noticed that Pin and Michel were talking to each other and took Pin away as he was the principal accused and was not supposed to communicate with anyone. Pin could not get off to sleep; he was used to being beaten and that did not frighten him very much, but he was in an agony of doubt about the best line to take up at the interrogation. He would have loved to revenge himself on Michel and the others and tell the Germans straight away that he had given the pistol to the men in the tavern, and also that they had formed a *Gap*; but to turn into an informer would be another irreparable action, like stealing the pistol; it would mean he would never be stood another drink at the tavern, or be able to sing or listen to dirty stories there. And then he might also involve that man Committee, who was always so glum and miserable, and Pin would have been sorry about that as Committee was the only decent man among the lot. Pin would like Committee to arrive now, all wrapped up in his raincoat, enter the interrogation room and say, '*I* told him to take the pistol.' That would be a fine gesture, worthy of Committee, and no harm would come to him for it either, for just as the S.S. were going to lead him off to prison, there would be a shout, like at the cinema, of: 'Here come our lads!' and Committee's men would rush in and set them all free.

When the German officer asks Pin about the belt he replies: 'I found it.' Then the officer takes up the belt and hits him over the cheek with all his strength. Pin reels and nearly falls; he feels as if bunches of needles had been stuck into all his freckles; the blood flows down his already swollen cheek.

His sister screams. Pin cannot help thinking how often she herself had hit him just as hard, and that now she's acting and just pretending to be sensitive. The Fascist interpreter leads his sister away, and the sailor begins some complicated speech in German, pointing at Pin, but the officer signs for him to be quiet. They ask Pin if he has decided to tell the truth; who sent him to steal the pistol?

'I took it to shoot at a cat, intending to bring it back,' says Pin, but he cannot manage to put an ingenuous expression on his face, which feels swollen all over. He is overwhelmed by a vague longing for affection.

Another blow on the other cheek, not so hard this time, though. Then Pin, remembering his method with the municipal guards, lets out a piercing shriek even before the belt has touched him, and goes on screaming. A scene begins with Pin jumping round the room, shrieking and sobbing, and the Germans running after him trying to catch him and hit him again, while he shouts protests and insults and wilder and wilder replies to the questions they continue to ask him.

'Where did you put that pistol?'

Now Pin can tell the truth: 'In the spiders' nests.'

'Where are they?'

Pin, deep down, would prefer to be friends with these people. The municipal guards also used to hit him first, and then start joking with him about his sister. If he could make friends with these men too it would be fine to explain to them where the spiders make their nests and arouse their interest and they'd come with him and he'd show them all the places. Then they would all go off to the tavern together and buy wine and move on later to his sister's room to drink, smoke, and watch her dance. But the Germans and Fascists, a beardless, blue-faced lot, don't seem people with whom any understanding is possible. They go on hitting Pin, so he will never tell them where the spiders make their nests; he has never told his friends, so why should he tell them?

Instead he begins giving great deep exaggerated sobs, like the sobs of a newborn baby, mingled with screams and curses and stamping of feet which can be heard all over the German headquarters. No, he won't betray Michel, Giraffe, Gian and the others; they are his real friends. Pin is now full of admiration for them because they are against these swine here. Michel can be sure Pin won't betray him, he must be hearing the screams and saying to himself: 'He's a lad of iron, Pin is, he's holding out and refusing to talk.'

In fact the noise Pin is making can be heard over the whole building; the officers in the other rooms begin complaining; there's always a coming and going for permits and supply contracts at the German headquarters, and it's not good that everyone should hear a child being beaten up too.

The officer with the baby face gets an order to stop the interrogation; he can go on another day and in a different place. But it is difficult to silence Pin now. They try to explain that it's all over, but their voices are drowned by his screams. Then a number of them cluster round him and try to calm him down, but he breaks away from them and screams louder than ever. Then they bring his sister in hoping she'll console him, and he nearly jumps up at her and bites her. After a time there's a whole group of Germans and of Fascist militiamen following

58

him around and trying to calm him down; one of them strokes his head, another tries to dry his tears.

Finally, exhausted, panting, his voice too hoarse to speak, Pin goes quiet. A militiaman is now detailed to take him off to prison and bring him back next day for more interrogation.

Pin comes out of the office with this armed militiaman following him; his face looks tiny under its thatch of hair, his eyes are squeezed dry and his freckles washed by tears.

On the threshold he meets Michel on his way out, a free man.

'Hallo, Pin,' says he, 'I'm going home. I'm joining up tomorrow.'

Pin frowns at him, his eyes red, his mouth open.

'Yes, I've asked to join the Black Brigade.[1] They've told me what the perks are and the pay they get. Then, you know, during round-ups you can snoop around people's houses and take what you want. Tomorrow they'll give me my weapons and uniform. Keep your chin up, Pin.'

The militiaman taking Pin to prison is wearing a black cap with a red *Fascio* embroidered on it. He's young and very short, with a rifle taller than himself. He's not one of the blue-shaven type of Fascists.

They have been walking along for five minutes and neither of them has yet opened his mouth.

Then, 'If you want to, you can get into the Black Brigade too,' the militiaman says to Pin.

'If I want to, I can get into that cow of a grandmother of yours,' Pin replies readily.

The militiaman pretends to be offended.

----

[1]The Black Brigades were formed by the Fascists early in 1944 to hunt members of the Resistance.

'Hey, who d'you think you're talking to? Hey, who taught you that?' and he stops.

'Go on, take me to the blasted prison, hurry up about it,' says Pin.

'Why, d'you think you'll be left quiet in prison? You'll be taken off for interrogation all the time, and beaten till you're bruised all over. D'you like being beaten?'

'You, on the other hand, should go to hell.'

'I'll send you to hell.'

'And I you, your father and your grandfather too,' says Pin.

The militiaman is a bit dim, and is outdone by Pin each time.

'If you don't want them to beat you, join the Black Brigade,' he says.

'And then?' says Pin.

'And then go out on round-ups.'

'Do *you* go out on round-ups?'

'No. I'm stuck at headquarters.'

'Liar. I wonder how many rebels you've killed and don't want to admit it.'

'I swear. Never been out on a round-up.'

'Except the ones you have been on.'

'Except the one they captured me on.'

'They captured you in a round-up too?'

'Yes, a fine round-up it was, really fine. Wiped up everyone, myself included. I was hiding in a chicken-coop. A really fine round-up, it was.'

Pin is annoyed with Michel, not because he thinks Michel has behaved badly and become a traitor. What annoys Pin is getting it wrong every time and never being able to foresee what grown-ups will do next. When one of them seems to be thinking in one way, Pin finds he's thinking in another; he can never foresee what the changes will be.

Pin, in his heart of hearts, feels he'd like to be in the Black Brigade too, and go around all hung with Fascist badges and tommy-guns, terrifying people and being treated by the grown-ups as one of them, linked together by the barrier of hatred separating them from other men. Perhaps, thinking it over, he *will* decide to go into the Black Brigade; at least he could get the pistol and perhaps be allowed to keep it and carry it about openly on his uniform; and then he could also get his own back on the German officer and the Fascist sergeant by making fools of them, and take his revenge in jeers for all the sobs and screams.

There is a song of the Black Brigade which goes: *And they call us the scamps of Mussolini . . .* followed by various obscenities. The Black Brigade can sing obscene songs in the streets because they are 'the scamps of Mussolini'; that's wonderful, thinks Pin. But this militiaman is a fool and gets on Pin's nerves, so he replies rudely to everything he says.

The prison is in a big villa requisitioned from English owners, for the old fortress down on the port is being used by the Germans as an anti-aircraft post. It is a strange villa, in the middle of a wood of monkey-puzzle trees, and must have looked like a prison even before, with its turrets and terraces and chimney-pots turning in the wind, and all the railings that were there before as well as those added since.

Now the rooms are used as cells, strange cells indeed with parquet and linoleum floors, great walled-up marble fireplaces, and basins and bidets stopped up with rags. There are armed sentries on the turrets, and on the terraces the prisoners queue up for their rations, then scatter for their daily airing.

It is feeding time when Pin arrives, and suddenly he realizes that he's very hungry. They give him a bowl too and put him in the queue.

Many of the prisoners are in for evading the call-up, and

also for various infringements of war-time restrictions, such as unlicensed slaughtering of animals or trafficking in petrol or pounds sterling. Nowadays there are very few ordinary criminals, for no one bothers about thieves; those there have past sentences to serve and are too old to ask to be called up and get them remitted. The political prisoners can be distinguished by the bruises on their faces and by their awkward movements on bones broken during interrogation.

Pin is a 'political' too; it shows at once. He's eating his soup, when up comes a big heavily built youth with a face even more livid and swollen than Pin's, and shaven hair under a peaked cap.

'They've fixed you nicely, comrade,' he says.

Pin looks at him, not knowing how to treat him yet.

'And you too,' he says.

The youth with the shaven head says, 'They interrogate me every day and beat me up with a whip made of gristle.'

He says this very grandly, as if they were doing him a special honour.

'If you want my soup, here you are,' he says to Pin. 'I can't eat it, as my throat's full of blood.'

And he spits out a reddish froth on to the ground. Pin looks at him with interest; he has always had a strange admiration for anyone who manages to spit blood, and always liked to see someone with tuberculosis spitting.

'Then you've got T.B.,' he says to the shaven youth.

'They may have given me T.B.,' agrees the other importantly. Pin looks at him admiringly; perhaps they'll become real friends. He has also given Pin his soup and that pleases Pin very much because he's hungry.

'If they go on like this,' says the youth with the shaven head, 'they'll ruin me for life.'

Pin says: 'Then why don't you join the Black Brigade?'

The youth with the shaven head gets up then and stares at him from his swollen eyes: 'Hey, d'you know who I am?'

'No, who are you?' exclaims Pin.

'Have you ever heard of Red Wolf?'

Red Wolf! Who hasn't heard of Red Wolf? Every time there's an attack against the Fascists, at every bomb that explodes in one of their headquarters, at every spy who vanishes without anyone knowing what has happened to him, people whisper the name of Red Wolf. Pin also knows that Red Wolf is sixteen years old and used to work at the 'Todt'[1] as a mechanic; others who'd worked at the 'Todt' to avoid the call-up had told Pin about him and how he wore a Russian-style cap and always talked about Lenin and how he'd been nicknamed KGB. He also had a passion for dynamite and time-bombs and had, it seemed, gone into the 'Todt' to learn how to make mines. Then one day the railway bridge blew up and KGB did not appear at the 'Todt' any more; he was in the mountains and came down into the town at night, carrying a big pistol and wearing a white, red, and green star on his Russian-style cap. He had let his hair grow long and now called himself Red Wolf.

And now here was Red Wolf standing in front of him, with his Russian-style cap which no longer had a star on it, his big head shaved, his eyes swollen, and spitting blood.

'Yes, are you him?' asks Pin.

'I am,' says Red Wolf.

'And when did they take you?'

'Thursday on the Borgo bridge; armed and with the star on my cap.'

---

[1]The German Todt organization was responsible for building defences, and Italian workers in it were exempted from military service.

'And what will they do to you?'

'Perhaps,' he says with his air of importance, 'perhaps they'll shoot me.'

'When?'

'Perhaps tomorrow.'

'What're you going to do?'

Red Wolf spits blood on the ground. 'Who are you?' he asks Pin. Pin gives his name. He has always wanted to meet Red Wolf, to see him appear one night in the alleys of the Old Town, but Pin has always been a little afraid of him, because of that sister of his who goes with Germans.

'Why are you here?' asks Red Wolf, in a tone almost as peremptory as the Fascists during an interrogation.

Now it is Pin's turn to give himself airs.

'I stole a pistol from a German.'

Red Wolf gives him a look of approval, then asks in a serious voice:

'Are you in the partisans?' Pin says, 'No.'

'You're not organized? Not in a *Gap*?'

Pin is delighted to hear that word again. 'Yes, yes,' he says, '*Gap*!'

'Who're you with?'

Pin thinks a little, then says: 'With Committee.'

'Who?'

'Committee. Don't you know him?' Pin tries to put on a superior air, but it doesn't work. 'A thin man, with a light-coloured raincoat.'

'You're lying. The committee is made up of lots of people, and no one knows who they are. They're preparing the rising. You don't know anything.'

'If no one knows who they are, you don't either.'

Pin doesn't like talking to boys of Red Wolf's age because

they always try to be superior and never take him into their confidence but treat him like a child.

'I do know,' says Red Wolf, 'I'm one of the *Sim*.'[1]

Another mysterious word. *Sim*! *Gap*! What a lot of words there must be; Pin wishes he knew them all.

'I know all about you, though,' he says, 'I know that you are also called KGB.'

'That's not true,' says Red Wolf, 'you mustn't call me that.'

'Why not?'

'Because we're not out for social revolution now, but for national liberation. When Italy's been liberated by the people, then we'll nail the bourgeoisie down to their responsibilities.'

'What?'

'Just that. We'll nail the bourgeoisie down to their responsibilities. The brigade commissar explained it all to me.'

'D'you know who my sister is?' The question has nothing to do with what they are saying, but Pin is tired of talking of things he knows nothing about and prefers to get back to his usual subjects.

'No,' says Red Wolf.

'The Dark Girl of Long Alley.'

'Who's she?'

'What d'you mean, who's she? Everyone knows my sister. The Dark Girl of Long Alley.'

It seems incredible that a youth like Red Wolf has never heard of his sister. In the Old Town children of six are already beginning to talk about her and telling girls of the same age what she does when she's in bed with a man.

'Hey, he doesn't know who my sister is. That's a good one . . .'

---

[1] *Servizio Informazione Militare* – Military Intelligence Service – the term could apply to either side.

Pin would like to call the other prisoners round and begin his usual clowning.

'I don't even look at women at the moment,' says Red Wolf, 'there'll be time after the rising . . .'

'But suppose they shoot you tomorrow?' says Pin.

'We'll just see who gets it in first, them shooting me or me shooting them.'

'What d'you mean?'

Red Wolf thinks a little, then leans over and whispers in Pin's ear:

'I've got a plan and if it comes off I'll have escaped by tomorrow, and then I'll make all these Fascist swine pay one by one for beating me up.'

'Escape? Where to?'

'Back to the detachment. To Biondo's. And we'll organize an action that will really make them sit up.'

'Will you take me with you?'

'No.'

'Please, Wolfy, take me with you.'

'My name is Red Wolf,' says the other. 'When the commissar told me that KGB wasn't a good name I asked him what I could call myself and he said "Wolf". Then I told him that I wanted a name with something red in it because the wolf's a Fascist animal, and he said: "Then call yourself Red Wolf."'

'Red Wolf,' says Pin. 'Listen, Red Wolf; why don't you want to take me with you?'

'Because you're only a child, that's why.'

From the beginning, ever since Pin and Red Wolf had talked about the stolen pistol, Pin had felt that they could become real friends. But now here is Red Wolf treating him like a child again and that gets on Pin's nerves. With other youths of Red Wolf's age Pin can at least assume superior airs by talking about women, but this subject does

66

not seem to work with him. But how fine it would be to go around in a band with Red Wolf and make explosives big enough to blow up bridges and walk through towns firing machine-gun bursts against patrols. It might even be better than the Black Brigade. Only the Black Brigade wears a death's head as a badge, and that makes more of a show than a tricolour star.

It seems quite unreal to be standing there talking to someone who may be shot next day, to be on that terrace full of men crouching on the ground over their food, under chimney-pots turning in the wind and warders watching from turrets with machine-guns trained. It's like some enchanted play, surrounded by that park full of the black shadows of those strange pines. Pin has almost forgotten his beating, and is beginning to wonder whether it's all a dream.

Now the warders are getting the prisoners in line before returning to their cells.

'Where's your cell?' Red Wolf asks Pin.

'I don't know where they'll put me,' says Pin, 'I haven't been in yet.'

'I'd like to know where you are,' says Red Wolf.

'Why?' asks Pin.

'You'll see.'

Pin is always irritated by people who keep on saying: 'You'll see.'

But suddenly, in the line of prisoners beginning to march away, he thinks he has seen a face he knows, knows very well indeed.

'Say, Red Wolf, d'you know that man ahead, the one who's so thin and walks in that strange way . . . ?'

'He's an ordinary criminal. Leave him alone. They aren't to be trusted, ordinary criminals.'

'Why not? I know him!'

'They are proletarians without class-consciousness,' says Red Wolf.

CHAPTER FOUR

'Pietromagro!'

'Pin!'

When a warder takes him to his cell and opens the door Pin gives a cry of surprise; he'd been right about the prisoner he saw on the terrace, the one who walked in that odd way; it really was Pietromagro.

'D'you know him?' asks the warder.

'Bloody hell do I not! He's my boss!'

'Good. Then the whole firm has been relocated here,' says the warder, and locks the door. Pietromagro had been inside a month or two, but to Pin, seeing him, it seems that years have passed. He's all skin and bone, yellow skin covered with hair and hanging from his neck in flabby folds. He is sitting on a heap of straw in a corner of the cell, with his stick-like arms along his sides. When he sees Pin he raises them. Up to now Pin's only relations with his boss have been shouts and blows; but now, finding him here in this state, he feels a mixture of pleasure and pity.

Pietromagro even speaks differently: 'Pin! You here too, Pin!' he says in a hoarse, wailing tone, without any curses at all; and it's plain that he too is pleased to see Pin. He takes him by the wrists, but not in the way he always did before, to twist them; and looks at him from yellow eyes. 'I'm ill,' he says, 'I'm very ill, Pin. These swine here won't send me to the infirmary. I don't understand what's going on here; the place is full of nothing but political prisoners and one day they'll end by mistaking me for a "political" and putting me up against a wall.'

'They beat me,' says Pin, and shows the marks.

'Then you're a "political" too,' exclaims Pietromagro.

'Yes, yes,' says Pin. 'A political.'

Pietromagro thinks this over. 'Of course, of course, a "political". I'd begun to think, seeing you here, that you'd started a career as a jail-bird. For once you get into prison you're never away from it long; as soon as you're freed you get put back in again. But of course if you're a "political" it's a different thing. Why, if I'd known more as a young man I'd have become a "political" too. Ordinary crimes don't get you anywhere; steal a little and you go to prison, steal a lot and you end up with villas and palaces. But commit a political crime, and though you go inside just the same – in fact whoever does anything ends up in prison – it's at least with a hope of a better world, without prisons, one day. That's what I was told by a "political" who was in prison with me years ago, a man with a black beard. He's dead now. For I've known every kind of convict, ordinary ones, smugglers, tax-evaders; but I've never known any as decent as the "politicals".'

Pin cannot quite grasp the meaning of this speech but he feels sorry for Pietromagro and stands quietly looking at the veins swelling and ebbing on his neck.

'Now, you see, I'm ill. I can't piss. I need treatment, instead of which here I am lying on the ground. I haven't blood running in my veins any more, but yellow piss. I can't drink wine, and I long to get drunk for a week. The penal code's all wrong, Pin; it lists everything you mustn't do in life, stealing, murdering, receiving stolen goods, but it doesn't say a word about what you *should* do instead of all that, when you find yourself in certain situations. Pin, are you listening to me?'

Pin looks at his yellow face which is hairy like a dog's and feels his breath panting over him.

'Pin, I'm going to die. You must swear to do something. Say "I swear" to what I'm going to say. "I swear that I'll fight all my life long to do away with prisons and to rewrite the penal code." Now say "I swear".'

'I swear,' says Pin.

'Will you remember, Pin?'

'Yes, Pietromagro,' says Pin.

'Now come and help me catch my lice,' says Pietromagro. 'I'm full of them. D'you know how to crack 'em?'

'Yes,' says Pin. Pietromagro begins looking inside his shirt, then hands Pin a corner of it.

'Have a good look in the seams,' he says. Catching Pietromagro's lice is not much fun, but Pin feels sorry for the poor man, with his veins full of piss and without perhaps much longer to live.

'And the shop, how's the shop going?' asks Pietromagro. Neither apprentice nor master has ever liked his job much; but now they begin discussing the work still to be done, the price of leather and thread, and who will mend shoes for the neighbourhood now that both of them are in prison. Soon they are sitting on the straw in a corner of the cell, cracking lice and talking about welting and soling, stitching and heeling without ever abusing their jobs, which has never happened in their whole lives.

'Say, Pietromagro,' exclaims Pin, 'why don't we set up as a cobbler in prison, to mend the prisoners' shoes?'

This has never occurred to Pietromagro, who used to go to prison quite willingly once so as to eat without working. But now he rather takes to the idea; perhaps if he could work he wouldn't feel so ill.

'I can ask. Will you come in on it?'

Yes, Pin will come in on it; working in these circumstances would be something new, something they had thought up for themselves, as amusing as a game. And being in prison wouldn't be too unpleasant, with Pietromagro who wouldn't hit him any more, and singing songs to the prisoners and warders.

At that moment a warder opens the door, and outside is Red Wolf, who is pointing at Pin and saying: 'Yes, that's the one I mean.'

The warder calls him out and locks up the cell, leaving Pietromagro all alone inside. Pin cannot understand what they want.

'Come along,' says Red Wolf, 'you must give me a hand with carrying down a barrel of refuse.'

Just along the passage, in fact, there stands an iron barrel full of refuse. Pin thinks how cruel it is to make Red Wolf, who is in such a bad state from his beatings, do heavy work with only a child like himself to help him. The barrel is so high it reaches Red Wolf's chest and so heavy it's difficult to lift. While they are trying to lift it Red Wolf brushes Pin's ear with his lips and whispers: 'Now keep a sharp look-out, this is our chance,' then out loud: 'I've been asking for you all round the cells, I need your help.'

This is wonderful, Pin thinks, he never dared hope for such a thing. But Pin soon gets attached to places he is in, and even prison, he finds, has its attractions; perhaps he would like to escape with Red Wolf a little later, when he's spent a little time here, but not just when he's arrived.

'I'll do it by myself,' says Red Wolf to the warders, who are helping him lift the barrel on to his shoulders. 'I just need the boy to steady it behind so it doesn't tip over.'

They start moving, with Red Wolf bent double under the weight and Pin holding the iron barrel straight by one end.

'D'you know the way?' the warders shout after him. 'Careful not to fall down the stairs.'

As soon as Red Wolf has turned the first landing he asks Pin to help him rest the barrel on a window-ledge. Is he already tired? No, Red Wolf wants to talk to him. 'Now listen carefully. When we reach the lower terrace you're to go ahead and begin talking to the sentry. You must hold his attention so that he doesn't take his eyes off you; you're small and he'll have to keep his head down to talk to you, but don't get too near him, you understand?'

'And what will you do?'

'I'll put a helmet on him. Mussolini's helmet. You'll see. D'you understand what you're to do?'

'Yes,' says Pin, who has not understood anything yet, 'and what then?'

'I'll tell you later. Just a moment. Open your hands.'

Red Wolf pulls out a piece of soap and rubs it over the palms of Pin's hands, then over his legs, particularly inside the knees.

'Why?' asks Pin.

'You'll see,' says Red Wolf, 'I've studied my plan in every detail.'

Red Wolf belongs to the generation brought up on boys' coloured adventure albums; only he has taken them all seriously and life has not disproved them so far. Pin helps him lift the barrel back on to his shoulder, then when they reach the terrace, goes on ahead to talk to the sentry.

The sentry is standing by a balustrade, looking sadly over the trees; Pin goes toward him with his hands in his pockets, feeling in his element again; his old bravado of the alley has returned.

'Hallo,' says he.

'Hallo,' says the sentry.

It's a face Pin has never seen before; a sad southerner with cheeks all hacked about from shaving.

'Hell, fancy seeing you here!' exclaims Pin. 'I was just saying to myself, where's that old bastard got to, when I see you there in front of me.'

The sad southerner looks at him, trying to prise open his half-shut lids. 'What? Who're you?'

'Hell, you're not going to tell me you don't know my sister?'

The sentry mutters something about not knowing anyone. 'Are you a prisoner? I can't talk to prisoners.'

And Red Wolf hasn't arrived yet!

'Don't you tell me ...' says Pin. 'You mean to say that since you've been here you've never had a dark girl with curly hair?'

The sentry looks perplexed.

'Yes, as a matter of fact, I have. What about her?'

'A girl who lives in an alley round the corner of the right of a square behind a church then up some steps?'

The sentry blinks. 'What?'

Pin is thinking: 'I bet it'll turn out he really has been with her!' By now Red Wolf should be there: maybe he can't carry the barrel on his own?

'I'll just explain,' says Pin. 'D'you know where the market square is?'

'Mmmm ...' says the sentry, and begins looking away; it's not working, he must find something more interesting, but if Red Wolf doesn't arrive soon everything will be wasted.

'Wait,' says Pin. The sentry turns his eyes back at him for a moment.

'I've got a photograph in my pocket. I'll show it to you in a minute. Only a bit of it, though. Just the head or you won't sleep tonight.'

The sentry is now leaning over him, and has even succeeded in completely opening both eyes, the eyes of some cave-dwelling animal. Then finally Red Wolf appears at the entrance to the terrace; although bent double under the barrel of refuse, he is managing to walk on the tips of his toes. Pin pulls both hands out of one of his pockets and waves them in the air, as if he were concealing something: 'Ha! Ha! You'd like to see it, eh?'

Red Wolf is drawing nearer, with long silent steps. Then Pin begins to slide one hand over the other, very slowly. Red Wolf is now right behind the sentry. The sentry is looking at Pin's hands; they are soapy; why? and where's this photo anyway? Then all of a sudden a stream of refuse falls on the sentry's head; and not only refuse, but something hard comes crashing down all round him; he's suffocating, he can't free himself; he's caught, and his rifle with him. Then he falls down and feels himself turning and rolling along the terrace.

Meanwhile Red Wolf and Pin have already jumped over the balustrade.

'There,' Red Wolf says to Pin, 'hang on there and don't let go,' and he points at a drain-pipe. Pin is frightened, but Red Wolf has already almost flung him out into the empty air, and he is forced to grip the drain-pipe. Now he is slithering on his soapy hands and knees; it's rather like sliding down bannisters, only much more frightening; whatever he does he mustn't look down or let go of the drain-pipe.

Red Wolf on the other hand has leapt out into space. Is he trying to kill himself? No, he's trying to reach the branches of a monkey-puzzle tree not far away, and hang on to them. But the branches break off in his hands and he falls with a crash of twigs and a shower of pine-needles. Pin feels the ground getting nearer beneath him, and is not sure if he is more frightened for himself or for Red Wolf, who might have killed himself. He touches the ground, nearly breaking his legs, and there at the foot of the pine tree sees Red Wolf lying on the ground under a heap of little branches.

'Wolfy. Are you all right?' he calls.

Red Wolf raises his face, and the bruises from his interrogation are now indistinguishable from those of his fall. He glances around. There is a sound of firing.

'Run for it,' says Red Wolf.

He gets up and begins running, with a limp.

'Run for it,' he repeats. 'This way!'

Red Wolf knows where to go and leads Pin through the abandoned park, full of wild creepers and spiky weeds. Shots are fired at them from the tower, but the park is so thick with conifer trees and bushes that there is cover everywhere. Even so Pin is not quite sure if he has been hit or not, as he knows you don't feel a wound at once, then suddenly you drop down dead. Red Wolf leads him through a little gate, through an old greenhouse, then makes him climb a wall.

Suddenly the shadows of the park dissolve, and before them opens a scene in brilliant light and primary colours, like a child's transfer. They have a moment of panic and drop to the ground; in front of them stretches a bare hillside, and all round it, vast and calm, the sea.

Then they go into a field of carnations, crawling through them so as not to be seen by women in big straw hats watering among the geometric patterns of grey stalks. Behind a big cement water-tank near a pile of folded mats used to cover the carnations in winter to prevent them freezing, there is a hollow.

'In there,' says Red Wolf. They crouch down behind the water-tank and pull the mats round them so that they can't be seen.

'We'll have to wait here till dark,' says Red Wolf.

Pin suddenly remembers himself hanging on the drain-pipe and the sentries shooting, and goes into a cold sweat.

Such things are almost more terrifying to remember than to live through; but you can't feel really frightened with Red Wolf near. It's wonderful to be sitting with him behind the water-tank; like playing hide-and-seek; except that there is no difference between the game and real life, and it has to be played seriously, which Pin likes.

'Are you hurt, Red Wolf?'

'Not much,' says Red Wolf, passing a finger wet with saliva over his cuts. 'The branches broke my fall when they cracked off. I had it all thought out. How did you get on, with that soap?'

'Bloody hell, Red Wolf, you really are amazing. How d'you know all these things?'

'A Communist must know everything,' replies the other. 'A Communist must know how to act in all situations.'

He's amazing, thinks Pin, a pity he can never resist showing off.

'There's only one thing I'm sorry about,' says Red Wolf. 'Being unarmed. I'd give anything for a Sten.'

Sten; another mysterious word; *Sten, Gap, Sim*, how can anyone ever remember them all? But this last remark of Red Wolf's has filled Pin with delight; now he can show off, too.

'I'm not worried about that myself,' says he, 'I've got a pistol and no one else can touch it.'

Red Wolf frowns at him, trying not to show too much interest.

'You've got a pistol?'

'Hm, hm,' says Pin.

'What calibre? What make?'

'A real pistol. A German sailor's. I stole it from him. That's why I was put inside.'

'Tell me what it's like.'

Pin tries to explain, and Red Wolf describes every existing

type of pistol and decides that Pin's is a P.38. Pin is enthusiastic; pee thirty-eight, what a lovely name, pee thirty-eight!

'Where've you got it?' asks Red Wolf.

'In a certain place,' says Pin.

Pin has to decide now whether or not to tell Red Wolf about the spiders' nests. Red Wolf is certainly an amazing fellow who can do all kinds of extraordinary things; but the place where spiders make their nests is a very great secret and must be kept among real close friends. Pin is not sure, in spite of everything, if he really likes Red Wolf; he is too different from all the others, grown-ups and boys too; he is always saying serious things and takes no interest in his sister. But in spite of that, if Red Wolf took an interest in the spiders' nests, Pin would like him very much. Pin, in his heart, cannot understand why all grown-up men concern themselves so much with his sister, who has teeth like a horse and arm-pits full of black hair; but grown-ups never seem to talk to him without making some remark about her, and Pin has become convinced she must be important and that he himself is important because he's the brother of the Dark Girl of Long Alley. But he is sure too that the spiders' nests are more interesting than his sister and than all this male and female business, though he can never find anyone else who realizes it; if he did find someone he would even forgive a lack of interest in the Dark Girl.

'I know a place,' he says to Red Wolf, 'where spiders make their nests.'

'*I* want to know,' replies Red Wolf, 'where you've got the P.38.'

'Well, it's there,' says Pin.

'Describe it to me.'

'D'you want to know what spiders' nests are like?'

'I want that pistol.'

'Why? It's mine.'

'You're only a child, interested in spiders' nests, what can you do with a pistol?'

'It's mine, hell, and if I want to I'll throw it in the river.'

'You're a capitalist,' says Red Wolf. 'Capitalists argue like that.'

'Oh, go and hang yourself,' says Pin.

Red Wolf says, 'Are you mad talking so loud? If they hear us we're done for.'

He moves away from Red Wolf and they lie there in silence for a time. No, it's hopeless, Pin thinks; Red Wolf has saved him from prison, but they can't ever be friends. But he is frightened of being left alone, and this business of the pistol binds him with a double link to Red Wolf, so he mustn't burn his boats.

Now he sees that Red Wolf has found a piece of charcoal and is beginning to write something on the cement side of the water-tank. Pin also takes up a bit of charcoal and begins drawing dirty pictures; once he had covered all the walls of the alley with such dirty drawings that the parish priest of San Giuseppe complained to the *Comune* and had them repainted. But Red Wolf is intent on his writing and takes no notice of him.

'What are you writing?' asks Pin.

'Death to Nazis and Fascists,' says Red Wolf. 'We mustn't waste our time. Here's a chance to do a little propaganda. Take some charcoal and write too.'

'I *have*,' says Pin, and points to his obscene drawings. Red Wolf is furious and begins to rub them out.

'You mad? Fine propaganda that'll make.'

'But what's the use of making propaganda here? Who d'you think will come and read anything here except lizards?'

'Shut up. I thought of putting arrows on the water-tank, then on the wall, as far as the road. People will follow the arrows to here and read this.'

78

This is another of the games which only Red Wolf knows how to play; they are very complicated and absorbing games, but they don't make you laugh.

'What shall I write then? "Long Live Lenin"?'

Years ago in the alley there had been some graffiti which appeared regularly on a wall and went: Long Live Lenin. The Fascists would come and rub it out and it was back again next day. Then one day they arrested Fransè the carpenter and the writing never appeared again. People said Fransè had died on an island.

'Write: "Long Live Italy", "Long Live the Allies",' says Red Wolf.

Pin does not enjoy writing. At school the mistress – how crooked her legs were, seen from under the bench – used to hit him over the fingers. The W for 'Viva' is very difficult to write properly: better find some easier word. Pin thinks a moment, then begins: A-R-S-E.

The days are beginning to lengthen and dusk never seems to come. Every now and again Red Wolf looks at one of his hands; it acts as a watch; every time he looks at it he sees it getting darker; when he can only see a black shadow it will mean that it's dark enough for them to come out. He and Pin have made up their quarrel and Pin has decided that he will take him to the path of the spiders' nests, to dig the pistol up. Red Wolf gets to his feet; it's dark enough now. 'Are we going?' asks Pin.

'Wait,' says Red Wolf, 'I'll go and have a look around and then come back for you. One is less dangerous than two.'

Pin doesn't want to stay alone, but he is also afraid of coming into the open without knowing what's there.

'Say, Red Wolf,' he exclaims, 'you won't just leave me alone here?'

'Trust me,' says Red Wolf, 'I'll give you my word to come back. Then we'll go and look for the P.38.'

Now Pin is all alone, waiting. With Red Wolf no longer there every shadow takes on a strange shape, every noise sounds like a footstep coming nearer. It's the sailor cursing in German at the top of the alley and now coming to look for him, naked except for his vest, and saying that Pin has also stolen his trousers. It's the baby-faced officer with a police-dog on a lead, whipping it with the belt of the pistol. The face of the police-dog is like that interpreter's with the rat-like moustache. They have got to a chicken-coop and Pin is afraid that it's he himself who is hiding inside there. But they go in, and find the militiaman who took Pin off to prison, crouching down like a chicken, for some unknown reason.

Then Pin thinks that a familiar face is peering into his hiding-place and smiling at him. It's Michel the Frenchman! But Michel puts his cap on and his smile changes into a nasty grin; it's the cap of the Black Brigade with the death's head on it! Now Red Wolf is coming at last! But no, a man with a light-coloured raincoat joins Red Wolf, takes him by an elbow and shakes his head, pointing at Pin, with a dissatisfied look; it's Committee! Why doesn't he want Red Wolf to join Pin? Committee points at the drawings on the water-tank, huge drawings representing Pin's sister in bed with a German. Behind the tank there is a heap of manure. Pin had not noticed it before. Now he tries to scoop himself out a hiding-place in the middle of the manure, but as he does so he touches a human face; a man is buried alive in the manure, it's the sentry with the sad face and the cheeks hacked about from shaving!

Suddenly, with a start, Pin wakes up. How long has he been asleep? Around him now it is pitch dark. Why has Red Wolf not returned yet? Has he met a patrol and been captured? Or can he have returned and called him as he slept and then gone off thinking Pin was no longer there? Or perhaps there was a search for them both going on in the country around, and Red Wolf could not move a step?

Pin comes out from behind the water-tank. The croaking of frogs seems to echo from the great wide throat of the sky, the sea to be a huge shining sword in the depths of the night. Being out in the open gives Pin a strange sense of smallness, not of fear. He is alone now, alone in the whole world. He walks off through the serried rows of carnations and of *calendule*, then makes for the higher slopes of the hills, to keep above the military area. Later he will come down to the river-bed and the paths which are his own.

He's hungry. The cherries are ripe at this season. Here's a tree, far from any house. Has it grown there by magic? Pin climbs up into the branches and begins to pick the cherries carefully. A big bird takes flight almost in his hands; it was sleeping in the branches. Pin at that moment feels a friend of everything and wishes he had not disturbed it.

When he has taken the edge off his hunger he fills his pockets with cherries and climbs down from the tree, then walks on again spitting out cherry-stones. Then he thinks the Fascists might follow the track of the stones and catch him up. But no one in all the world would be clever enough to think of a thing like that, no one except Red Wolf! Yes, if Pin leaves a trail of cherry-stones, Red Wolf will manage to find him, wherever he is! All he has to do is to drop a cherry-stone every twenty yards. There, he'll eat a cherry the other side of that wall, then another past that old olive-press, and another after the medlar tree; and so on until he reaches the path of the spiders' nests. But long before he has reached the river-bed the cherries are finished. Then Pin realizes that Red Wolf will never find him again.

Now he is walking along in the bed of the torrent, which is almost dry, among big white stones and bamboos rustling like paper. Down at the bottom of the pools are sleeping eels as long as human arms, to be caught by hand, sometimes, when you drain water off. Where the torrent opens out in the Old Town, shut up now like a pine-cone, sleep drunken men and women satiated with love-making. Pin's sister is asleep alone or perhaps in company; she has already forgotten him, no longer wondering if he is alive or dead. Lying awake, dying, all alone on the straw of his cell, is Pin's master, Pietromagro, the blood turning yellow with urine in his veins.

Pin has now reached his own area; there is the irrigation channel, there is the path with the nests in it. He recognizes the stones, he looks to see if the earth has been disturbed. No, nothing has moved. He scoops with his hands, with almost forced anxiety; touching the holster gives him a soothing sensation, like a baby feeling a toy under its pillow. He takes the pistol out and passes his finger over the hollows to take the earth out. Out of the barrel, very quickly, jumps a tiny spider; it had made itself a nest inside!

It's lovely, his pistol is, the only thing he has in all the world now. He grasps it and imagines he is Red Wolf, tries to think what Red Wolf would do if he had this pistol in his hand. But that reminds him that he is alone, and that he can't go to anyone for help, neither to those double-faced incomprehensible men at the tavern nor to his traitress of a sister nor even to Pietromagro in prison. He doesn't even know what to do with that pistol, nor how to load it; if he's found with it in his hand they'll certainly kill him. He puts it back in its holster and covers it with stones and earth and grass again. Now there is nothing left for him to do but wander aimlessly about the countryside. He hasn't the slightest idea what to do.

He begins walking along the irrigation channels again; in the dark it's easy to lose one's balance on them and put a foot in the water or fall on to the allotment beneath. Pin concentrates every thought on keeping his balance; it may, he thinks, hold in the tears pressing at the back of his eyes. But the tears well over and cloud his pupils and soak his eyelashes. First they flow silently, then pour down, while sobs hammer at the back of his throat. As he walks along crying like that, a big human shadow comes towards him along the channels. Pin stops, and the man stops too.

'Who goes there?' says the man.

Pin does not know what reply to make, his tears are welling up more than ever and now he's broken into deep, desperate sobbing.

The man comes nearer; he is large and tall, dressed in civilian clothes and armed with a tommy-gun, and has a cloak strapped over his shoulder.

'Hey, why are you crying?' he says.

Pin looks at him; he is a huge man with a flat face like one of those masks which spout water in fountains; he has spreading moustaches and very few teeth.

'What're you doing here, at this time of night?' says the man. 'Are you lost?'

The oddest thing about the man is his cap, a woollen one with an embroidered edge and a pom-pom at the top, of some indistinguishable colour.

'You *are* lost. I can't take you back home, as I've nothing to do with any homes nowadays and can't take lost children back to theirs!'

He says all this almost in a tone of self-justification, more to himself than to Pin.

'I'm not lost,' says Pin.

'Well, what are you doing wandering about here?' says the big man with the woollen cap.

'First you tell me what you're doing.'

'Fine,' says the man, 'you're a bright lad, you are. As you're

83

so bright, why are you crying? I go round at night, killing people. Are you afraid?'

'No. Are you a murderer?'

'There, you see, not even children are afraid any more of men who go around killing people. No, I'm not a murderer, but I kill people all the same.'

'Are you going to kill someone now?'

'No. I'm on my way back.'

Pin is not frightened of him, for he knows that some men who kill others are good guys all the same; Red Wolf is always talking about killing and yet he is a good guy; the painter who lived opposite killed his wife and yet he was a good guy; Michel the Frenchman has probably killed people by now and yet he will always be the same Frenchman Michel! Then the big man with the woollen cap begins talking about killing, in a sad voice as if he did it as a penance.

'D'you know Red Wolf?' asks Pin.

'Of course I do. Red Wolf is one of Biondo's lot. I'm with Dritto. How d'you know him?'

'I was with him, with Red Wolf, and I've lost him. We escaped from prison. We shoved a barrel over the sentry. First they beat me with the belt of the pistol. I'd stolen it from the sailor who goes with my sister. My sister is the Dark Girl of Long Alley.'

The big man with the woollen cap is running a finger over his moustaches. 'Yes . . . yes . . . yes . . . yes . . .' he says, trying to understand the story all at once. 'And now where d'you intend going?'

'I don't know,' says Pin. 'Where are you going?'

'I'm going to the camp.'

'Will you take me with you?' says Pin.

'Come along. Have you had anything to eat?'

'Cherries,' says Pin.

'Alright. Here's some bread,' and he pulls a piece of bread out of his pocket and hands it to Pin.

They set off and walk through an olive-grove. Pin chews the bread; a tear or two is still falling over his cheek and he swallows it with the bread. The big man has taken him by the hand; it's a huge hand, warm and soft, and seems made of bread too.

'Well! now, let's see what happened . . . Behind it all, you said, there was a woman . . .'

'My sister. The Dark Girl of Long Alley,' says Pin.

'Of course, behind all the stories with a bad ending there's always a woman, make no mistake about that. You're young, just listen to what I tell you. War's all the fault of women . . .'

CHAPTER FIVE

Pin awakes to see such bright stretches of sky between branches of woodland trees that it almost hurts him to look up. It is day, a day serene and free, with birds singing.

The big man is standing beside him rolling up the cloak which he has just taken off Pin's back.

'Quick, let's be off, it's day,' he says. They had walked almost all night, clambering up through olive-groves, then scrub-land, and eventually into dark pine-woods. They had seen owls, too; but Pin was never afraid because the big man with the little woollen cap always held his hand.

'You're dropping with sleep, son,' the big man had said, as he pulled him along behind him. 'You don't want me to carry you, do you?'

Pin had in fact had great difficulty in keeping his eyes open, and would have sunk happily into the mass of ferns in the undergrowth till they covered him right over. It had been almost morning when they reached the open space near a charcoal burner's hut and the big man said, 'We can halt here.'

Pin had stretched out on the coal-blackened ground, and watched, as if in a dream, the big man cover him with his cloak, then go to and fro with bits of wood, break them up, and light a fire.

Now it is day, and the big man is pissing on the embers of the fire; Pin gets up and does the same beside him. Standing there he looks up at the big man's face; he has not yet seen it properly in the light. As the shadows melt away in the woods and from his eyes still gluey with sleep, Pin keeps on making new discoveries about him. He's younger than he'd seemed and his proportions more normal; his moustache is reddish-colour and he has blue eyes, his face is like a grotesque mask because of the gaps in his teeth and a flattened nose running across his face.

'We'll soon be there now,' he says to Pin now and again, as they walk on through the woods. He does not talk much and Pin enjoys walking beside him in silence; he is a little frightened, in his heart, of this man who goes round alone at night killing people, and then is so good and protective with him. Pin has always been embarrassed by good people; he does not know how to treat them and always longs to make fun of them and see how they react. But he feels different with the big man with the woollen cap, for he's a person who has done a lot of killing and can allow himself to be good without regrets.

The big man talks about nothing but how endless the war is and how after seven years with the Alpine troops he still has to go round with a gun and how the only people who are well-off these days are the women and how he'd been round every country and realized that women everywhere are all thoroughly bad lots. Most of this does not interest Pin, it's the sort of thing everyone says these days; but he has never heard anyone talk like that about women before. It's not as if this man is like Red Wolf who just isn't interested in women; he seems to know them well, but to have some personal motive for this attitude.

Now they have left the pines behind and are walking through chestnut woods.

'Very soon now,' says the big man, 'we really will be there.'

And just after that they meet a mule, with no other harness but a bridle, wandering about on its own, munching leaves.

'That's not the way to let a mule out, loose like that,' says the man. 'Here, Corsair, here my pretty.'

He takes it by the bridle and draws it along behind him. Corsair is a mangy old mule, docile and submissive. Meanwhile they have reached a clearing in the woods, with a hut in it for smoking chestnuts. There is not a soul to be seen. The man stops and so does Pin.

'What's up?' exclaims the man. 'Have they all left?'

Pin realizes that perhaps he ought to feel frightened, but he does not know how things are and so feels no fear.

'Hey! Who goes there!' says the man, not very loud, and slipping the tommy-gun from his shoulder.

Then from the hut appears a little man carrying a sack. He sees them, throws the sack down on the ground and begins clapping his hands. 'Hallo! Hey! Cousin! It's music day to-day!' he exclaims.

'Mancino!' exclaims Pin's companion. 'Where the hell are the others?'

The little man comes toward them, rubbing his hands.

'Three trucks, three loaded trucks, driving up the main road.

87

They were seen this morning and the whole battalion has gone out to attack them. Soon the music'll begin.'

He is a tiny little man, dressed in a big sailor's jerkin and with a cap made of rabbit fur on his bald head. Pin thinks he must be a gnome living in this hut in the middle of the woods.

The big man runs a finger over his moustache. 'Good,' he says, 'I must go down and have a shot too.'

'If you're still in time,' says the little man. 'I've stayed behind to get the food ready. I'm sure they'll have already put 'em out of action by midday and are now on their way back.'

'You might have looked after the mule too, as you were here,' says the other. 'If I hadn't come across it, it'd have ended on the seashore.'

The little man ties up the mule, then looks at Pin.

'And who's this? Have you had a son, Cousin?'

'I'd die rather than have kids,' says the big man. 'This lad was working with Red Wolf and got lost.'

That is not exactly the way it was, but Pin is pleased to be introduced in such a way and perhaps the big man said it on purpose to show him in a good light.

'Here, Pin,' says the big man, 'this is Mancino, the cook of the detachment. You must treat him with respect, as he's old, and if you don't he won't give you an extra ration of soup.'

'Listen, my little recruit of the revolution,' says Mancino, 'd'you know how to peel potatoes?'

Pin would like to bring out some obscenity in reply, just to make friends, but he cannot think of a suitable one on the spur of the moment, and answers: 'Yes, I do.'

'Good, an assistant cook is just what I need,' says Mancino. 'Wait and I'll go and fetch the knives,' and he vanishes into the hut.

'Hey, is he your cousin?' Pin asks the big man.

'No, everyone calls me Cousin.'

'Me too?'

'You too what?'

'Can call you Cousin?'

'Of course; it's a name like any other.'

Pin likes this. He tries it out at once. 'Cousin!' he calls.

'What d'you want?'

'Cousin, what are the trucks coming up for?'

'To have our guts, that's what they're coming for. But we'll go out and have theirs. That's life.'

'Are you going too, Cousin?'

'Of course, I must go.'

'Aren't you tired of walking?'

'I've been walking and sleeping with my boots on for the last seven years. When I die, it'll be with my boots on.'

'Seven years without taking your boots off. God, Cousin, how your feet must stink.'

Meanwhile Mancino has returned. But he is not only carrying the knives for the potatoes. On his shoulder is perched a large ugly bird, chained by a claw like a parrot, and fluttering its clipped wings.

'What is it? What is it?' exclaims Pin, who has already put a finger under its beak. The bird rolls its yellow eyes and nearly pecks it.

'Ah! Ah!' grins Mancino. 'He'll have your finger off in a second! Be careful. Babeuf's a spiteful old hawk!'

'Where did you get him, Mancino?' asks Pin, who is learning more and more not to trust either grown-ups or their pets.

'Babeuf is a veteran partisan. I got him from his nest when he was tiny; now he's the mascot of the unit.'

'You'd have done better to let him free as a bird of prey,' says Cousin. 'Some mascot: he brings worse luck than a priest.'

But Mancino has put a hand to his ear and signed to them to be quiet.

'Did you hear that? Ta . . . Tata . . . ?'

They listen. Firing can be heard from down the valley. Bursts of fire, ta . . . pum, and an occasional boom of hand grenades.

Mancino bangs a fist against his palm, with that harsh little laugh of his: 'That's it! It's started! I'm telling you, today we'll wipe out the lot of them.'

'Well, we won't wipe out much if we stay here. I'm going to have a look,' says Cousin.

'Wait a bit,' says Mancino, 'eat a few chestnuts first. There were some left over this morning. Giglia!'

Cousin raises his head with a jerk. 'Who are you calling?' he asks.

'My wife,' says Mancino, 'she arrived last night. The Black Brigade were hunting for her down in the town.'

A woman has now appeared on the threshold of the hut; she has peroxided hair and is still young, though a little over-blown.

Cousin is frowning and smoothing his moustache with a finger.

'Hallo, Cousin,' calls the woman, 'I've been evacuated up here,' and she saunters towards him with her hands in her pockets; she's wearing long trousers and a man's shirt.

Cousin gives Pin a glance. Pin understands: things will end badly if they start bringing women up here. Pin is proud to share secrets with Cousin, secrets about women, exchanged by glances.

'You've brought good weather with you,' says Cousin rather sourly, looking away and pointing towards the valley, from which firing can still be heard.

'What weather could be better than this!' exclaims Mancino. 'Just listen to the noise of the heavy machine-guns. Do you hear the racket of those flamethrowers? Giglia, give him a handful of chestnuts as he wants to go down.'

Giglia looks at Cousin with a strange smile. Pin notices that her eyes are green and her neck ripples like the back of a cat.

'There's no time,' says Cousin, 'I must go. Get the food ready. Good luck, Pin.'

And off he goes, with the rolled cloak strapped to his back and the tommy-gun still in his hands.

Pin would like to run after Cousin and stay with him, but he is aching all over after all his adventures, and also he finds the firing down in the valley makes him vaguely apprehensive.

'And who are you, baby?' says Giglia, running a hand over his thatch of scruffy hair, though Pin draws his head away as he has never been able to stand women's caresses; also he doesn't like being called 'baby'.

'Your little son! Didn't you notice last night that you were having a baby?'

'A good answer! A good answer!' croaks Mancino, rubbing the knives against each other and driving the hawk into a frenzy. 'One should never ask a partisan who he is. The reply is "I'm a son of the proletariat, my country is the International, my sister is the Revolution."'

Pin winks, and looks at him out of the corner of his eye: 'What's that? You know my sister too?'

'Don't take any notice of him,' says Giglia. 'He has bored everyone with his talk about perpetual revolution, even the commissars are against him. A Trotskyist, that's what they call him, a Trotskyist!'

Trotskyist; another new word!

'What does it mean?' he asks.

'I'm not sure what it means myself,' says Giglia, 'but it's a word that suits him: Trotskyist!'

'Stupid fool!' Mancino shouts at her. 'I'm not a Trotskyist!

If you've come up here to annoy me, you can go straight back to the town and get yourself captured by the Black Brigade!'

'Selfish swine!' replies Giglia. 'It's your fault . . .'

'Stop,' says Mancino, 'let me listen. Why isn't the heavy artillery firing any more?'

In fact the artillery, which has been firing continuous bursts up till now, has suddenly stopped.

Mancino gives his wife a worried look: 'What can have happened? Has the ammunition run out?'

'. . . or the machine-gunner been killed . . .' says Giglia apprehensively. They both stand there listening intently, then look at each other again and the spite comes back into their faces.

'Well?' says Mancino.

'I was just saying,' Giglia begins shouting again, 'that it's your fault I've had to live with my heart in my mouth for the last two months, and you still don't want me up here.'

'Bitch!' says Mancino, 'bitch! One of the reasons I came up here was . . . There! It's started again!'

The heavy artillery is firing again; short bursts, with long pauses in between.

'That's better,' says Giglia.

'. . . one of the reasons I came up here was,' shouts the other, 'that I couldn't stand living with you any longer, after all I saw you getting up to!'

'Oh yes? Then what about after the war's over and the merchant-ships sail again and I'll only see you two or three times a year? . . . Hey, what are those shots?'

Mancino listens, worried: 'They sound like mortars . . .'

'Ours or theirs?'

'Let me listen. There's one firing. It's theirs!'

'It's not firing. It's exploding, farther down the valley. It's ours . . .'

'Always contradicting! Curse the day I met you! Yes, they really are ours . . . Just as well, Giglia, just as well . . .'

'I told you so. A Trotskyist, that's what you are; a Trotskyist! Opportunist! Traitor! Filthy Menshevik!'

Pin is thoroughly enjoying himself; he feels at home. In the alley there were quarrels between husbands and wives that lasted for whole days, and he used to spend hours under their windows listening to them without missing a single word, as if they were on the wireless; and every now and again he would intervene with some comment of his own, shouted at the top of his voice, so that the litigants would sometimes break off, then both appear at the window-sill to swear at him.

It's all much better up here; in the middle of woods, to the accompaniment of firing, and with all these new colourful words.

Then suddenly everything is calm; in the valley the battle seems to have died down; and the husband and wife are staring furiously at each other, without a breath left in their throats.

'Hell, you aren't giving up so soon?' asks Pin. 'Have you lost the thread?'

They both look at Pin, then at each other to see which is going to speak, so as to contradict at once.

'They're singing!' exclaims Pin. Now from down in the valley comes the faint echo of a song.

'In German . . .' mutters the cook.

'Idiot!' shouts the woman. 'Can't you hear it's *Bandiera Rossa*?'

'*Bandiera Rossa*?' the little man claps his hands and gives a twirl in the air, while the hawk tries to fly above his head with its clipped wings. 'Yes; it's *Bandiera Rossa*.'

He begins running down the slope, singing: '*Bandiera Rossa la trionferà*,'[1] until he gets to the edge of a bluff, where he stops and listens.

---

[1] Lit. 'The Red Flag will triumph.'

93

'Yes. It's *Bandiera Rossa!*'

He comes running back with shouts of delight, the hawk planing behind him on its chain like a toy kite. He kisses his wife, claps Pin on the shoulder, and all three take hands and sing: '*Bandiera Rossa la trionferà.*'

'You see,' Mancino says to Pin, 'you mustn't get the idea that we were having a serious quarrel; it was all a joke.'

'That's right,' says Giglia, 'my husband is a bit silly but he's the best husband in the world.'

So saying she raises his rabbit-fur cap and kisses him on his bald pate. Pin cannot tell if they are lying or not, grown-ups are always so double-faced, but anyway he has enjoyed himself very much.

'Let's get down to peeling the potatoes,' says Mancino, 'they'll be back in a couple of hours and won't find anything ready.'

They turn out the sack of potatoes and sit round peeling them and throwing them in a pail. The potatoes are cold and freeze Pin's fingers, but it's pleasant to be peeling potatoes in the company of this strange little gnome who might be good or bad, and of his wife who is even more incomprehensible. But Giglia soon stops peeling and begins combing her hair. This annoys Pin who does not like working with someone lazing in front of him. But Mancino goes on peeling the potatoes; perhaps he's used to this, it's what always happens with them.

'What's there to eat today?' asks Pin.

'Goat's meat and potatoes,' replies Mancino. 'D'you like goat's meat and potatoes?'

All Pin knows is that he's hungry, and he says yes.

'You cook well, do you, Mancino?' he asks.

'Hell,' says Mancino, 'it's my job. Twenty years, I've spent, cooking on ships; ships of every kind and every nationality.'

'Pirate ships too?' asks Pin.

'Yes, pirate ships too.'

'Chinese ships too?'

'Chinese ships too.'

'Can you speak Chinese?'

'I can speak every language under the sun. And I know how they cook in every country under the sun; Chinese cooking, Mexican cooking, Turkish cooking . . .'

'How are you cooking the goat's meat and potatoes today?'

'Eskimo style. D'you like goat à l'Eskimo?'

'Hell, Mancino, goat à l'Eskimo!'

Pin now sees that Mancino has a drawing of a butterfly on the skin of one of his ankles, showing below his ragged trousers.

'What's that?' he asks.

'A tattoo,' says Mancino.

'What's it for?'

'You ask too many questions.'

When the first men arrive the water is just on the boil.

Pin has always wanted to set eyes on partisans. Now he is standing open-mouthed in the middle of the clearing in front of the hut, and no sooner has he begun staring at one of them than another two or three arrive, all looking different and all hung with weapons and machine-gun belts.

They might even be soldiers, a company of soldiers who had disappeared during a war many years ago and been wandering in the forests ever since without finding their way back, their uniforms in rags, their boots falling to pieces, their hair and their beards all matted, carrying weapons which now they only use to kill wild animals.

They are tired and coated all over with sweat and dust. Pin had expected them to arrive singing; instead of which they are looking

95

grim and serious, and throw themselves on the straw in silence.

Mancino is skipping round them like a dog, beating his fist against the palm of his hands, and giving great hoots of laughter: 'We've given 'em a good hiding this time! How did we do it? Tell me about it.'

The men shake their heads; they are lying about on the straw and not speaking. Why are they so discontented? They look as if they'd returned from a defeat.

'Well? Did things go badly? Have we had many killed?' Mancino goes round saying from one to the other, completely nonplussed.

Now Dritto, the commander, arrives. He is a thin young man, with eyes framed in long black lashes and curious movements of the nostrils. He goes round swearing at the men and complaining because the food is not ready.

'Come on now; what's happened?' insists the cook. 'Didn't we win? If you don't tell me I won't do any more cooking.'

'Yes, yes, of course we won,' says Dritto, 'two trucks captured, twenty Germans killed; a good haul.'

He says this in a tone of irritation, as if he were being forced to admit it.

'Then did we have lots of killed too?'

'Two wounded in the other detachment. We're all intact, of course.'

Mancino looks at him; he is beginning to understand.

'Don't you realize they sent us over to the other side of the valley,' shouts Dritto, 'so we couldn't fire a shot! They'll have to make up their minds at Brigade headquarters; either not to trust the detachment and break it up; or to consider us partisans like all the others and send us into action. Another time if we're just put on rearguard duties we won't move. And I'll resign. Anyway I'm ill.' He spits and goes into the hut.

Cousin has now arrived and calls Pin.

'Pin, d'you want to see the battalion passing? Go down there, you can see the road from the edge of the ridge.'

Pin plunges down through the thickets and leans out beyond them. Below him he sees the road, with a line of men walking along it. They look different from all the others he has seen till now; brightly coloured, gleaming, bearded men, armed to the teeth, wearing the strangest uniforms; wide hats, helmets, leather jackets, bare chests, red scarves, bits of uniform from every army under the sun; and all· their weapons are different and all of them unknown to Pin. Some pale, glum prisoners also pass. Pin thinks all this is too good to be true, that it must all be due to the sun reflecting on the dusty road.

Suddenly he gives a start; he's seen a face he knows. There's no doubt of it; Red Wolf. He calls him and they soon join each other. Red Wolf has a German weapon on his shoulder and is limping on a swollen ankle. He is still wearing his Russian cap, but now it has a star on it, a red star with a white and green circle inside it.

'Fine,' he calls to Pin, 'you've got here by yourself; you're a bright lad.'

'God, Red Wolf,' says Pin, 'how on earth did you get here? I waited so long for you.'

'Well, you see, when I left you I thought I'd have a look at the place the Germans park their vehicles near there. I got into a garden nearby and from a terrace I saw soldiers fully equipped and getting ready to move. I said to myself, they must be mounting an attack on us: if they're getting ready now, they'll be up our way by dawn. So I ran all the way up here to warn them, and everything's turned out all right. But I twisted my ankle, the one that was so swollen when I fell that time, and now I'm lame.'

'You're amazing, Red Wolf, you really are,' says Pin, 'but you're a swine all the same to leave me when you'd given me your word of honour.'

'Honour,' he says, 'is due to the Cause first.'

Meanwhile they have reached Dritto's camp. Red Wolf looks all the men up and down and replies coldly to their greetings.

'You've got into fine company,' says he.

'Why?' asks Pin, a little bitterly; he has grown fond of these people already and does not want Red Wolf to come and take him away again.

Red Wolf whispers in his ear. 'Don't tell anyone; but this is what I've heard. They send the duds to Dritto's detachment, the cast-offs from the brigade. They may keep you here, because you're a child. But if you like I can try and get you moved.'

Pin does not like the idea of being kept here because he's a child; but the men he knows are not duds.

'Tell me, Red Wolf, is Cousin a dud?'

'Cousin is a man who has to be left on his own. He always goes round alone and is a good man and has guts. Seems there was some story about a woman he was in love with, last winter, who ended up causing the deaths of three of our men. Everyone knows it's not his fault, but it still niggles him.'

'What about Mancino? Is it true he's a *Trotskyist*?'

Perhaps, thinks Pin, he'll explain what that means.

'He's a Trotskyist, he's an extremist, the commissar of the brigade told me so. You don't agree with him, do you?'

'No, no,' replies Pin. Who knows? Perhaps *Trotskyist* means something degrading.

'Comrade Red Wolf,' exclaims Mancino, coming up with his hawk on his shoulder. 'We'll make you Commissar of the Soviet of the Old Town!'

Red Wolf does not even look him in the face. 'Extremism: Communism's infantile disorder,' he says to Pin.

CHAPTER SIX

Under the trees of the wood the ground is thick with chestnut husks and dried up pools full of hard leaves. In the evenings layers of mist spread between the trunks of the chestnut trees and shroud their bases, covered with the reddish sheen of moss and the bluish marks of lichen. The encampment can be sensed before it is reached, from the smoke rising above the tree-tops and the faint singing of a chorus, growing louder as one goes deeper into the woods. The hut is made of stone, two stories high, the lower storey with an earthen floor for animals, and the one above, made of logs, for shepherds to sleep in.

Now there are men above and below, sleeping on piles of fresh bracken and hay; as there are no windows through which the smoke of the fire on the ground floor can escape, it curls round under the slate roof and burns the eyes and throats of the men forcing them to cough. Every night the men crouch round the fire, lit under cover in case it is seen by the enemy, and crowd up together, with Pin in the midst of them, lit by flickering flames and singing away at the top of his voice as he used to in the tavern in the alley. The men look rather like the men of the tavern too, sitting there with hard eyes and splaying elbows, though they are not gazing resignedly into purple glasses; their hands are on the barrels of their weapons and tomorrow they will be going out to fire them against other men; against the enemy!

It is this that makes them different from others, this that gives

Pin a feeling new to him, that he has never felt before; it's their having enemies. In the alley there was shouting and rowing and insulting between men and women going on night and day, but there was never this bitter longing to meet the enemy, a longing which keeps these men awake at night. Pin does not yet realize what it means, to have enemies. To Pin there's something as disgusting as worms about all human beings; and something good and warm, too, which draws him to their company.

But these men can think of nothing but the enemy; they're like lovers; when they say certain words their beards quiver, their eyes glisten, and their hands stroke the barrels of their rifles. They do not ask Pin to sing songs about love or comic songs that make them laugh; what they want are songs full of bloodshed and violence, or others about prison and crimes which only Pin knows, or others so obscene that they have to be shouted out with hatred. Yes, these men fill Pin with more admiration than any others ever have: their stories are all about lorry-loads of men slaughtered and spies executed naked in ditches.

Below the hut the woods straggle off into strips of meadow, and there, it is said, spies are buried; Pin is a little afraid of passing that way at night, in case he feels a tug at his heels from hands growing up through the grass.

Pin is now accepted as one of the band; he is in everyone's confidence and knows the right phrase to make fun of each man, or get them to chase him, or tease them, or make them lash out.

'Hell, chief,' he says to Dritto, 'they say you've got your uniform all ready for when you leave the hills, with badges of rank, spurs and sword.'

Although Pin jokes with the leaders, he always tries to keep on the right side of them, for he likes to be in with them in case he can get off guard duty or some other job.

Dritto is a thin, young man, the son of emigrants from Southern Italy; he has the smile of a sick man, and lids always lowered over his long lashes. He is a waiter by profession; not a bad profession as one lives with the rich and only works alternate seasons; but he would much prefer to lie in the sun all the year round, with his thin muscular arms behind his head. Instead of which there is some demon in him which keeps him perpetually on the move and makes his nostrils quiver like antennae and gives him a subtle pleasure in handling weapons. They are doubtful about him at brigade headquarters as he has had unfavourable reports from the Committee, for he always wants to act on his own in battle and is too fond of giving orders and not fond enough of setting an example. But he can be brave when he wants to be and there are not many men capable of leadership available; so he has been given this detachment, which is considered unreliable, and useful mainly to dump men who might harm others. Dritto is offended about this and inclined to play up to brigade headquarters; every now and again he says he is ill and spends entire days lying on the fresh bracken in the hut, with his arms behind his head and his long lashes lowered over his eyes.

The detachment needs a good commissar to keep its leader on the right lines; but the commissar, Giacinto, is perpetually tortured by lice, which he has allowed to spread all over him and which he can no longer hold in check, so that he is beyond exercising any authority either over the commander or the men. Every now and again he is called to battalion or brigade headquarters to report on the situation and discuss means of dealing with it; but it is all wasted breath, for as soon as he gets back he starts scratching again from morning till night, and pretends not to notice what the commander is doing or what the men are saying about him.

Dritto takes Pin's jokes with a quiver of the nostrils and that sick smile of his, and says Pin is the best man in the detachment and that as he himself is ill and wants to resign they might as well put Pin in command, for things are bound to go wrong anyway. Then the men all turn on Pin and ask him when he is coming into action with them and if he can aim and fire at a German. This makes Pin angry, for in his heart he knows he would be frightened to be in the middle of shooting and is not even sure if he would be capable of firing at a man. But when he's surrounded by these comrades he tries to convince himself that he is like them, and begins describing what he will do when he's allowed to go into battle, holding his fists under his eyes as if he were firing a machine-gun.

This excites him; he thinks of the Fascists and when they beat him and of these bluish and hairless faces at the interrogation; ta-tatata, they're all dead, chewing the carpet under the German officer's desk, with bleeding gums. He too feels that sharp rasping urge to kill, even to kill the militiaman hiding in the chicken-coop, stupid though he is, perhaps just because he is stupid, to kill the gloomy sentry at the prison too, gloomy though he is, just because he is gloomy and his face is all hacked about from shaving. The urge is remote, vague, like the urge to love; it has an exciting and unpleasant taste like cigarettes or wine, an urge which all men have, he can't understand why, and which if satisfied would probably be pleasurable in some secret, mysterious way.

'If I was a boy like you,' says Long Zena, 'I'd nip straight down into town, shoot an officer, then escape up here again. No one would take any notice of a boy like you and you could get right under their noses. It would be easy for you to escape, too.'

Pin gets furious; he knows they say these things to make fun of him, and then won't give him any weapon or let him leave the camp.

'Send me,' he says, 'and I'll go, you'll see.'

'All right, go tomorrow,' they say.

'How much d'you bet that I'll go down and do in an officer, one day?'

'Come on, Dritto,' say the others, 'you'll give him a weapon, won't you?'

'Pin is assistant-cook,' says Dritto, 'his weapons are a knife for the potatoes and a ladle.'

'To hell with all your weapons! Why, I've got a German naval pistol that's better than any of yours!'

'Really!' say the others. 'And where d'you keep it, at home? A naval pistol; it must be one of those water ones.'

Pin chews his lips; one day he'll go down and dig up the pistol, and do wonderful things with it that will astonish them all.

'What d'you bet I've got a P.38 hidden, somewhere only I know?'

'What kind of partisan are you, keeping arms hidden? Describe the place and we'll go and fetch it.'

'No, it's a place no one knows but me, and I won't tell anyone.'

'Why not?'

'Spiders make their nests there.'

'Oh, go on with you. Spiders never make nests. They're not swallows.'

'If you don't believe me, then give me one of your weapons.'

'We got our weapons for ourselves. We con-quer-ed them!'

'Hell, I conquered mine too. In my sister's room, while the guy was . . .'

The others laugh, they don't understand what he is talking about. Pin feels like going off with his pistol and being a partisan all on his own.

'What d'you bet I'll find your pistol for you, your P.38?'

The question is asked by a slim youth with a perpetual cold, the shadow of a moustache, and parched lips flecked with saliva, called Pelle. He is polishing the bolt on a gun, with a rag, very carefully.

'I'll bet your life you'll never find the place where spiders make their nests,' says Pin.

Pelle stops rubbing a second. 'Listen, you snot-nosed kid, I know that river-bed inch by inch, you can't even guess the number of girls I've had on those banks.'

Pelle's two passions are weapons and women. He won Pin's admiration by his knowing talk about the qualities of all the prostitutes in the town and by saying things about Pin's sister that suggested he knew her well too. Pin feels a mixture of attraction and repulsion for him, so thin, with that perpetual cold of his, forever telling stories about girls he has grabbed by the hair and tricked into going out into the fields and then had there, or about the new complicated weapons issued to the Black Brigade. Pelle is young but has been all over Italy camping with the Young Fascists, and he has always handled weapons and visited brothels, even before reaching the prescribed age.

'No one knows where the spiders' nests are except me,' says Pin.

Pelle laughs, showing his gums. 'I know,' he says, 'I'm going down into town now to get a tommy-gun from a Fascist's house, and I'll look for your pistol too.'

Pelle goes down into the town every now and again and returns loaded up with weapons; he always seems to know where there are hidden weapons and who has them, and risks capture every time in order to increase his armoury. Pin is uncertain if Pelle is telling the truth; perhaps Pelle is the great friend he has been seeking for so long, who knows all about women and pistols and spiders' nests too; but those reddish, cold-ridden eyes of his are frightening.

'And will you bring me it, if you find it?' asks Pin.

Pelle's grin is all gums: 'If I find it, I'll keep it for myself.'

It is difficult to get Pelle to give up any weapons; every day there are rows at the detachment about Pelle not being a good comrade and claiming to have owners' rights over all the weapons he's acquired. He had joined the Black Brigade before going into the partisans, so as to have a tommy-gun, and had gone round the town at night shooting at cats. Then he had deserted from the Black Brigade after emptying half their armoury; since then he had always gone back to the town at regular intervals and found strange new automatic weapons and grenades and pistols there. He often talks about the Black Brigade, painting it in diabolic colours, but always with a certain fascination. 'At the Brigade they say this . . . they do that . . .'

'All right, Dritto, I'm off, as we agreed,' says Pelle now, licking his lip and giving little sniffs.

The men are not supposed to go and come on their own as they feel like it, but Pelle's expeditions are always fruitful; he never returns empty-handed.

'I'll let you go for two days,' says Dritto, 'not more, d'you see? And don't do anything silly and get yourself captured.'

Pelle goes on licking his lips. 'I'll take the new Sten,' he says.

'No,' says Dritto, 'take the old Sten. We need the new one.'

The usual argument.

'The new Sten's mine,' says Pelle; 'I brought it here and I'll take it when I like.'

When Pelle grows quarrelsome his eyes get redder still as if he were about to burst into tears and his voice becomes even more nasal and stuffed-up. Dritto, on the other hand, is cold and inflexible, and gives only a quiver of the nostrils before opening his mouth.

'In that case you don't move,' he says.

Pelle begins a long complaint, boasting of his own merits and saying that if that's the way he's treated he'll leave the detachment and take all his weapons with him. Suddenly Dritto gives him a sharp slap on the face. 'You do just what I tell you, see?'

The others look on, approvingly; they have no more liking for Dritto than for Pelle, but are pleased to see their commander make himself respected.

Pelle stands there sniffing, with the red marks of fingers showing on his pale cheek.

'You'll pay for this,' he says. Then he turns and leaves.

It is misty outside. The men shrug their shoulders. Pelle has made scenes like that before and has always returned with another haul. Pin runs after him. 'Say, Pelle, my pistol, listen, that pistol . . .' he calls, not quite knowing what he wants to ask him. But Pelle has vanished and Pin's shouts are muffled in the mist. He returns among the others, who have straw in their hair and sour looks.

To liven up the atmosphere and get his own back for the way they made fun of him Pin begins jeering at those least able to defend themselves and who can most easily be laughed at. He settles on four Calabrians nicknamed Duke, Marquis, Count and Baron. They are brothers-in-law, who left their own village to come and marry four sisters from Calabria who had emigrated up here; they make a group on their own, under the leadership of Duke, who is the oldest and can get himself respected.

Duke wears a round fur cap pulled down over one cheekbone, and has straight moustaches on a square proud face. In his belt is a big Austrian pistol; this he pulls out and thrusts in the stomach of anyone who contradicts him, grunting some truculent phrase in his angry-sounding dialect, full of double consonants and strange endings: 'I dddon't gives a fffuck!'

Pin copies him. Then Duke, who cannot stand being jeered at, runs after him waving the Austrian pistol and shouting: 'I'll bbblow your bbbrains out! I'll rrrip your bbballs off!'

But Pin is taking the risk because he knows that the others are on his side and that it amuses them to make fun of the Calabrians; Marquis with a face like a sponge and hair low on his forehead; Count, thin and gloomy as a mulatto; and Baron, the youngest, with a big black peasant's hat, a swivel eye and a medal of the Virgin hanging from a button-hole. Duke's job had been slaughtering for the black market and whenever there is an animal to cut up he asks to do it; there is some dark blood-cult in him. Often they go off, all four of them, down towards the valley and the carnation plantations where the sisters, their wives, live. And there they have mysterious duels with the Black Brigade, ambushes and vendettas, as if they were waging, on their own, a war caused by ancient family feuds.

Sometimes, at night, Pin is told to be quiet by Long Zena, also known as Wooden-Beret, who has reached a good part in his book and wants to read it out loud. Long Zena spends entire days without leaving the hut, lying stretched out on the dirty straw, reading a big book called *Super-Thriller*, by the light of a little oil-lamp. He has even been known to take the book into action with him and go on reading it, leaning it on the magazine of the machine-gun, while waiting for the Germans to appear.

He reads out loud in a monotonous Genoese cadence; it's a story about men disappearing in a mysterious Chinatown. Dritto likes hearing him read and tells the others to keep quiet; Dritto has never in his life had the patience to read a book through, but once, when he was in prison, he had

107

spent hours and hours listening to an old convict reading *The Count of Monte Cristo* out loud and had enjoyed that very much.

But Pin cannot understand the pleasure of reading and is getting bored. He says: 'Hey, Long Zena, what will your wife say that night?'

'Which night?' asks Long Zena, who is not yet used to Pin's jokes.

'The first night you go to bed with her and spend the whole time reading!'

'Porcupine-face!' exclaims Long Zena.

'Bull-lips!' replies Pin. The Genoese has a long pale face with two enormous lips and pale eyes under the peak of a leather cap that's so stiff it might be made of wood. Long Zena gets angry and starts getting up. 'Why bull-lips? Why d'you call me bull-lips?'

'Bull-face!' repeats Pin again and again, keeping out of range of his huge hands.

Pin feels he can risk this as he knows that the Genoese will never make the effort to run after him, and will always decide after a bit to let Pin go on talking, and start reading again from where his big finger is holding the place. He is the laziest man in the whole brigade; though his shoulders are like a stevedore's he always has some excuse, on marches, for not carrying a load. One by one all the detachments had got rid of him until he's ended up in Dritto's.

'How cruel it is,' says Long Zena, 'that men have to work all their lives.'

But there are countries, such as America, where men can get rich without much effort; Long Zena will go off there as soon as the boats begin sailing again.

'Free enterprise, the secret of everything is free enterprise,' says he, stretching his long arms lying on the straw, moving his lips while spelling out the words with a finger, in the book describing life in that free happy country.

At night, when everyone is asleep in the straw, Long Zena folds back the page he has begun, shuts the book, blows out the oil-lamp and goes off to sleep with his cheek resting on the cover.

CHAPTER SEVEN

The dreams of the partisans are short and rare, dreams born of nights of hunger, linked to food which is always scarce and always to be divided among so many; dreams about chewing bits of bread and putting them away in drawers. Stray dogs must have dreams like that, about gnawing bones and burying them. Only when the men's stomachs are full, when the fire is lit, and there has not been too much marching the day before, can they dream of naked women and wake up in the morning with spirits free and soaring, with all the exhilaration of the start of a voyage.

Then the men lying in the straw begin to talk about their women, about those in the past and those in the future, to make plans for when the war is over, and to pass each other faded yellow photographs.

Giglia sleeps by the wall, the other side of her dumpy little bald husband. In the morning she listens to the men talking with so much yearning, and feels their glances slithering towards her like snakes in the straw. Then she gets up and goes out to the well to wash herself. The men remain in the darkness of the hut, thinking of her opening her shirt and soaping her breasts. Dritto, who has been silent throughout, gets up and goes out to wash too. The men swear at Pin for reading their thoughts and mocking them.

Pin feels among them as he felt among the men in the tavern, only this world is more brightly coloured, more savage, with these nights in the hay and those beards crawling with lice. There is something else which attracts and frightens Pin, apart from that absurd fixation about women which is common to all grown-ups; every now and again they return to the hut leading some yellow-faced man whom Pin has not seen before, and who looks around as if incapable of opening his eyes wide or of unlocking his jaws to ask something he longs to know.

The man goes docilely out with them, into the misty dry meadows that lie at the edge of the woods; no one ever sees him return, and sometimes his hat or jacket or nailed boots appear on someone else. Pin finds this fascinating and mysterious, and he tries every time to join the little group of men walking off into the fields; but they push him away with curses, and Pin is left jumping about in front of the hut and poking a broom made of ferns at the hawk, thinking meanwhile of the secret rites taking place in the misty damp grass.

One night, to play a trick on Pin, Dritto tells him that in the third field up the mountain there's a surprise for him.

'Bloody hell, Dritto, tell me what it is,' says Pin, bursting with curiosity, but at the same time feeling a hint of fear for those grey clearings in the dark.

'Just keep walking along that third field until you find it,' says Dritto, laughing a cruel laugh.

So then Pin walks on his own through the dark, with fear penetrating his bones like the dank mist. He follows the strip of field which lies in between outcrops of the mountain, and has by now lost sight of the glow of the fire visible through the door of the hut.

He manages to stop just in time: one step more and he would

110

have walked on it! Beneath him he sees a huge white shape sprawled over the field: a human body, already stiff, lying face down in the grass. Stunned, Pin stares at it: a black hand jumps out from the earth on to the corpse, slithers down its flesh, and tries to grab on to it like the hand of a drowning man. But it's not a hand: it's a toad; one of those toads that roam the fields by night and that is now leaping on to the belly of the dead man. With his hair standing on end and his heart in his mouth, Pin races as fast as he can from the field.

One day Duke returns to the camp after having gone off with his three brothers-in-law on one of those mysterious expeditions of theirs. He arrives wearing a black woollen scarf round his neck and carrying his fur cap in his hand.

'Comrades,' he says, 'they've killed my brother-in-law Marquis.'

The men come out of the hut and watch Count and Baron arriving, also wearing black woollen scarves round their necks, and carrying a stretcher made of vine poles and olive branches on which is lying the body of Marquis, killed by the Black Brigade in a field of carnations.

The brothers-in-law put the stretcher down in front of the hut and stand round it with their heads bare and their chins lowered. Then they notice the two prisoners. These are Fascist prisoners captured in an action the day before, who are standing there peeling potatoes, unkempt and with feet bare and torn uniforms where the badges had been ripped off, explaining for the hundredth time to anyone near them that they had only joined the Black Brigade because they were forced to.

Duke orders the two prisoners to take picks and spades, and carry the stretcher to the meadows, to bury their brother-in-law's body. They set off; the two Fascists carrying on their shoulders the stretcher of branches with the corpse on it, followed by the three brothers-in-law, Duke in the middle with the other two on each side of him. They are holding their caps in their left hands at the level of their hearts; Duke his round fur cap, Count a woollen balaclava, Baron his big peasant's hat; in the other hand each of them carries a pistol, cocked. A short way behind follow all the others, in silence.

Then Duke begins reciting the prayers for the dead; the Latin words sound heavy with anger in his mouth, like curses; the two brothers-in-law intone the responses, with their pistols still cocked and their caps held to their chests. The funeral advances through the fields, at a slow pace; Duke gives the Fascists a few sharp orders every now and again, to go slowly, to hold the stretcher level, and to turn; eventually he orders them to stop and begin digging a grave.

The others also stop, some distance away, and stand looking on. Beside the stretcher and the two digging Fascists stand the three Calabrian brothers-in-law, their heads still bare, still with their black woollen scarves and cocked pistols, saying Latin prayers. The Fascists work quickly; soon they have dug a deep trench and look up at the brothers-in-law.

'Keep digging,' says Duke.

'Deeper?' ask the Fascists.

'No, wider,' says Duke.

The Fascists go on digging and throwing up earth, making a trench two or three times wider.

'Enough,' says Duke.

The Fascists lower the body of Marquis into the middle of the trench; then climb out to throw earth on top.

'Down,' says Duke. 'Cover it from down there.'

The Fascists throw spadefuls of earth up on to the dead man until they are each standing in separate ditches with the corpse between them. Every now and again they turn round to see if

Duke will let them get up again, but he tells them to go on throwing earth on the body, earth which has already formed a high tomb above the corpse.

Then the others leave the brothers-in-law standing there with their bared heads and their cocked pistols; and the mist comes up, a thick mist that blurs outlines and muffles sound.

The story of the Calabrian's funeral, when brigade head-quarters found out, aroused considerable disapproval, and Giacinto the commissar was called once again to report. Meanwhile the men in the hut seem gripped by a wild exaggerated gaiety as they listen to the jokes of Pin, who, sparing the mourning brothers-in-law for that evening, has launched out against Long Zena.

Giglia is kneeling by the fire, handing bits of wood one by one to her husband, who is trying to coax up the flames; meanwhile she is following what's said and laughing and swivelling her green eyes around the room. And every time her eyes meet the shadowed ones of Dritto, she laughs and Dritto laughs too, that evil sick laugh of his, and they gaze fixedly at each other, until she lowers her eyes and looks serious again.

'Pin, stop a second,' says Giglia, 'and sing that song which goes: *Who is it knocking at my door . . . ?*'

Pin leaves the Genoese in peace and starts on her.

'Say, Giglia, who would *you* like to come knocking on your door?' asks Pin, 'when your husband's not at home!'

The cook raises his bald head, reddened by the heat of the fire, with the sour little laugh he gives when he is being made fun of: 'What I'd like is to see you come knocking at my door, with Duke behind you waving a big knife and saying, "I'll bbblow your bbbrains out!" and then I'd like to close the door in your face.'

But the attempt to bring in Duke again is a clumsy one and

does not work. Pin takes a step or two towards Mancino and says with a frown and a sideways grin: 'What, Mancino, you mean to say you really didn't notice that time?'

Mancino has learnt by now that it's best not to ask Pin what he means.

'No, I didn't, did you?' he replies, but gives his sour laugh, because he knows Pin won't spare him and that the others are hanging on his lips to hear what he'll come out with.

'That time after you'd been at sea a year and your wife had a baby and took it off to the orphanage and you came back and noticed nothing?'

The others, who have held their breaths till now, burst into roars of laughter and try to draw the cook on: 'Oh, Mancino, what happened? You never told us about that!'

Mancino laughs too, but sourly as a green lemon. 'Why?' he says to Pin. 'Did you meet the child when you were at the orphanage for bastards yourself?'

'That's enough,' says Giglia. 'Can't you say anything that isn't malicious, Pin? Now sing us that song; it's so lovely.'

'If I feel like it,' says Pin; 'I don't work to orders.'

Dritto gets slowly to his feet, stretching: 'Go on, Pin, sing that song she's told you to, or straight out you go on guard duty.'

Pin shakes the hair off his eyes and grins at him. 'Hey, let's hope the Germans don't come. The chief's feeling sentimental tonight.'

He is all ready to parry the expected blow; but Dritto is looking at Giglia from his shaded eyes, above the cook's big head. Pin then gets into position, with his chin up and his chest out, and begins:

Who is it knocking at my front door, at my front door?
Who is it knocking at my front door?

It is a wild haunting song which Pin learnt from an old woman down in the alley; perhaps it was sung once by story-tellers at fairs.

'Tis a Moorish captain with all his slaves, with all his slaves,
'Tis a Moorish captain with all his slaves.

'Firewood,' says Mancino, and reaches out a hand towards Giglia. She takes up a broom made of ferns, but Dritto holds a hand out over the cook's head and takes it.

Tell me, woman, where is your son, where is your son?
Tell me, woman, where is your son?

Mancino still has his hand out and Dritto is now burning the sticks. Then Giglia holds out a handful of millet leaves above her husband's head and her hand meets Dritto's. Pin is following their movements with attentive eyes as he goes on singing.

My son has gone to war and can't return, and can't return,
My son has gone to war and can't return.

Dritto has taken Giglia's hand with one of his, then seized the millet leaves in the other and thrown them on the fire; after which he lets go of her hand and they look at each other.

May he choke on the bread he eats, on the bread he eats,
May he choke on the bread he eats.

Pin is following every movement with eyes blazing; he is

115

throwing more and more into his singing at every couplet, as if his very soul were in it.

And may he drown in the water he drinks, in the water he drinks
And may he drown in the water he drinks.

Now Dritto is climbing over the cook and is near Giglia. Pin's voice thunders in his throat as if it would crack open.

May he be swallowed by the earth he treads, by the earth he treads.
May he be swallowed by the earth he treads.

Dritto is now crouching down by Giglia's side; she is handing him bits of wood and he is putting them on the fire. The others are all intent on the song, which has reached its most dramatic point.

Woman, what are you saying, for I am your son, for I am your son;
Woman, what are you saying, for I am your son!

The flames on the fire are too high now; some of the wood should be taken off, not more put on, or the hay on the floor above will catch fire. But Giglia and Dritto are still passing each other twigs and leaves.

Forgive me, son, for speaking ill of you, for speaking bad of you,
Forgive me, son, for speaking ill of you.

116

Pin is sweating from the heat, and trembling all over with the effort he is making; the last high note was so piercing that a flapping and raucous screech can be heard from under the dark roof; the hawk Babeuf has woken up.

He drew out his sword and cut off her head, cut off her head,
He drew out his sword and cut off her head.

Mancino has now put his hands on his knees, he has heard the hawk wake and is getting up to feed it.

Off went the head and spun into the hall, spun into the hall,
Off went the head and spun into the hall.

The cook always has a sack by him filled with intestines of slaughtered animals.

Now the hawk is perching on one of his fingers and Mancino is feeding bits of blood-red kidneys into its beak.

On the floor of that room will grow a beautiful flower, a beautiful flower,
On the floor of that room will grow a beautiful flower.

Pin draws in breath for the last lines. He moves near Dritto and Giglia and shouts almost into their ears:

The flower of a mother killed by her own son, killed by her own son,
The flower of a mother killed by her own son.

Pin flings himself to the ground, exhausted. Everyone breaks into applause. Babeuf squawks. At that moment there is a shout from the men sleeping above: 'Fire! Fire!'

The flames have grown into a huge bonfire, crackling and spreading over the hay covering the logs above.

'Out! Out!' The men are all stumbling about in confusion, snatching at weapons, boots, blankets, falling over others lying down.

Dritto has regained control of himself and jumped to his feet. 'Quick! Clear the place! First automatics and ammunition, then rifles. Last the sacks and blankets. And remember the rations!'

The men, some of whom were lying barefoot, are seized with panic, snatching at anything that comes to hand and flinging themselves at the door. Pin plunges in between their legs and opens himself a way out, then runs to find a place from which to admire the fire. What a wonderful sight it is!

Dritto has pulled his pistol out. 'No one leaves before everything's saved! Out with the things and go back! The first man I see making off I'll shoot!'

The flames are already licking the walls, but the men have got over their panic and are now leaping back into the middle of the flames and smoke to save the weapons and rations. Dritto enters too and shouts orders, coughing amid the smoke, then comes out again to call others and prevent their escaping. He finds Mancino in a bush with the hawk on his shoulders and all his belongings round him and with a kick orders him back to the hut to get the cooking-pot.

'Anyone I don't see going back will catch it from me!'

Giglia passes him, calmly going towards the fire, with that strange smile of hers. 'Keep away!' he mutters to her.

He's a perverse creature, is Dritto, but he has an instinct for command; he knows that the fire is his fault, caused by the irresponsibility to which he listlessly gives in; he knows that he will certainly be in serious trouble with his superiors, but now he is a leader again, his nostrils quivering as he directs the evacuation of the hut in the middle of the fire, dominating the confused rushing to and fro of the men caught by surprise while resting, who would have lost all the material as long as they saved themselves.

'Upstairs!' he shouts. 'There's still a machine-gun there and two haversacks of ammunition!'

'Can't get up there!' they reply, 'the floor's all on fire.'

Suddenly there is a shout: 'The floor's falling in! All outside!'

Now the first explosions can be heard – some grenades which had remained in the straw. Dritto shouts, 'All outside! Keep away from the hut! Take the stuff some way off, particularly the explosives!'

Pin, from his observation post on a mound, sees the fire break out into sudden bursts like fireworks and hears shots, even bursts of machine-gun fire, as the ammunition belts fall into the flames and explode, one cartridge after the other; from a distance it must sound like a battle. Sparks fly high into the sky, the tops of the chestnut trees seem tipped with gold; a branch first looks gilded then suddenly goes incandescent; the fire is spreading into the trees, it may soon burn up the whole wood.

Dritto is making a list of missing material: a Breda, six belts of ammunition, two rifles, lots of grenades, cartridges and a sackful of rice. His career is over: he will never command again; they may shoot him; yet his nostrils are still quivering, he goes on apportioning jobs out among the men, as if this were a routine evacuation.

'Where are we going?'

'I'll tell you later. Let's get out of the woods. Come on.'

The detachment, loaded with weapons and baggage, moves off through the meadows in single file. Mancino is carrying the cooking-pot on his back with Babeuf perching on top of it. Pin has charge of the other kitchen things. Now a rumour begins circulating among the men: 'The Germans have heard the shots and seen the fire, we'll soon have them on our heels.' Dritto turns an impassive yellow face towards them

'Silence! Not a word from anyone! Come on, walk!'

He might be organizing a retreat after an unsuccessful engagement.

CHAPTER EIGHT

The new camp is in a barn, where they are all crowded up on top of each other; the roof has fallen in and lets the rain through. In the morning they scatter to sun themselves among the rhododendrons on the rocky slopes around, lie on the frosty bushes and take off their shirts to look for lice.

Pin likes being sent off by Mancino on errands to places nearby, to fill pails for the cooking-pot at the spring, or gather wood among the burnt trees with a little hatchet, or fish out watercress from the stream for the cook's salads. Pin sings as he goes, looking at the sky and the clear morning world and the mountain butterflies of strange colours meandering over the meadows. Every time he keeps Mancino waiting impatiently while the fire goes out and the rice gets sticky, and each time he is cursed in every language under the sun when he arrives back, with his mouth full of strawberry juice and his eyes dancing with the fluttering of the butterflies. Then Pin becomes the little boy of Long Alley again, starting rows which go on for hours and draw the men away from the rhododendrons to collect round the kitchen fire.

But when he wanders along the paths in the mornings Pin forgets the old streets with their stagnant mule-urine, the odour of male and female in his sister's unmade bed, the sour smell from the squeezed trigger and smoke from the red, burning open gun-barrels, the swish of the belt during that interrogation. Now Pin has discovered all kinds of coloured things; yellow and brown mushrooms growing damp in the earth, red spiders on huge invisible nets, hares all legs and ears which appear suddenly on the path then leap zigzagging out of sight.

Yet a sudden fleeting thought is enough for Pin to get caught up again in the sickness of the hairy, ambivalent charnel-house of humanity; and, with eyes screwed up and freckles clustering, he watches the crickets making love, or thrusts pine needles in the puffy backs of little toads, or pees on an ant heap and watches the porous earth sizzle open and hundreds of little red and black ants scurry away through the mud.

Then the world of men draws him again, that world of incomprehensible men with their opaque looks and angry mouths. And he goes back to Mancino, the little man whose laughter is getting sourer and sourer, and who never leaves his cooking-pots to go into action but stays there while the hawk in a foul mood flaps its clipped wings on his shoulder.

But the most amazing thing about Mancino are his tattoos: he has them on every part of his body, tattoos of butterflies, sailing ships, hearts, hammers and sickles, Madonnas. One day Pin saw him while he was shitting and discovered he even had a tattoo on one of his buttocks: a man standing up seemed to be embraced by a woman on her knees.

Cousin is different; although he seems to be forever complaining and hinting that he is the only one who really feels the strain of war, he still goes round by himself with his tommy-gun on his shoulder, and every time he returns to camp sets off again a few hours later, always with that reluctant air of his as if he is only doing it because he has to.

Whenever there is a mission to be carried out, Dritto looks round and says: 'Who wants to go?'

Then Cousin shakes his big head as if he were the victim of an unjust fate, loads his tommy-gun on his shoulder, and goes off sighing; with that gentle face of his looking more than ever like the mask on a fountain.

Dritto sprawls among the rhododendrons with his arms behind his head and his gun between his knees, feeling sure that measures are being taken against him at brigade headquarters. The men's eyes are heavy with sleep above their matted beards; Dritto tries not to look at them as he feels their glances are full of silent resentment against him. But they still obey him, as if by mutual agreement, to avoid drifting to disaster. Yet he listens to everything, and every now and then gets up to give an order; he does not want the men to get out of the habit of thinking of him as their leader; if they do, even for a moment, he will have lost them.

The burning of the hut has never worried Pin; it was a wonderful fire and the new camp is surrounded by lovely places to explore. But he's a little frightened of going near Dritto; he wonders whether Dritto will try and put all the blame for the fire on to him, for distracting his attention by his singing.

Now Dritto is calling him: 'Pin, come here!'

Pin goes towards the sprawling Dritto, not daring to bring out any of his usual jokes; but he knows Dritto is hated and feared by the others and feels rather proud to be near him at that moment, almost as if he were an accomplice.

'D'you know how to clean a pistol?' asks Dritto.

'Well,' says Pin, 'you take it to bits and I'll clean the parts.'

Everyone is a little nervous of Pin, as they never know what he will say, but Dritto senses that today Pin will not mention the fire or Giglia or any of those things, so the boy is the only member of the band he can be with.

He spreads out a handkerchief and puts the pieces down on it as he dismembers the pistol. Pin asks if he can help to take it to pieces and Dritto shows him how. Pin enjoys sitting there talking to Dritto like this, in low voices and without either saying anything disagreeable to the other. He compares Dritto's pistol with his own buried one and talks about the parts that are different or better in both. And Dritto does not make the usual comment, that he doesn't believe Pin has a buried pistol; perhaps they all believe it, anyway, and only said they didn't to make fun of Pin; Dritto seems a nice man when Pin talks to him like this, and when he's explaining how the pistol works he becomes enthusiastic and no longer looks obsessed by evil thoughts. Even pistols, when talked about like this, no longer seem instruments for killing people, but strange enchanted toys.

The other men lie about looking angry and abstracted; they take no notice of Pin wandering round them and do not want to sing. It is bad when discouragement seeps into the men's bones like damp from the earth, and they no longer trust their leaders and feel they are already surrounded by Germans with flamethrowers among the rocks and rhododendrons and that they will have to flee from valley to valley and die one by one in this never-ending war. They begin discussing the war – when it started and who wanted it and when it would end, and if things would be better then or worse than before.

Pin does not know the difference between when there's war and when there isn't. He seems to have heard people talking about war ever since he was born, only the bombings and the black-out came later.

Every now and again aeroplanes pass over the mountains; you can look at their undersides, without escaping into tunnels as you have to in towns. Then far away towards the sea there is a deep roar of bombs dropping, and the men think of their homes which are perhaps in ruins at that moment and tell each other that the war will never end and how they can't understand who wanted it.

'I know who wanted it! I've seen them!' a man called Carabiniere suddenly says. 'It was the students!'

Carabiniere is even more ignorant than Duke and lazier than Long Zena; his father was a peasant who, realizing he would never get his son to wield a spade, said to him: 'Join the Carabinieri'; so the son joined and was given a black uniform with a white bandolier and carried out his duties in town and country without ever realizing what he was doing. After the 8th of September[1] he was told to arrest the parents of deserters, then one day he heard that he was going to be deported himself as he was for the King; so he escaped. First the partisans had wanted to make him dig his own grave, because of those parents of deserters he had arrested; then they realized that he was just a poor wretch and had sent him to Dritto's detachment, as no one wanted him in any of the others.

'In '40 I was in Naples and I know!' says Carabiniere. 'It was the students! They carried flags and placards and yelled "Malta and Gibraltar" and that they wanted five meals a day.'

'Shut up, you were a Carabiniere,' the others shout at him;

---

[1]On 8 September 1943 the announcement of the armistice between Italy and the Allies led to the period of the civil war and Resistance in Italy (1944–45).

'you were on their side and you went around delivering the red arrest warrants.'

Duke spits violently and touches his Austrian pistol. 'The Carabinieri are all pigs, swine and bastards!' he says between his teeth. In his part of the country there is a long history of struggle with the Carabinieri, of Carabinieri shot and killed by wayside shrines.

Carabiniere protests, panting and waving his big peasant hands in front of his tiny eyes and low forehead.

'Us Carabinieri were against them! Yes, sir, we were against the war the students wanted. We tried to keep them in order! But we were twenty to one against, so they had their war!'

Mancino is standing a little way off, looking as if he's on tenterhooks; he is stirring the rice in the cooking-pot; if he stops stirring for a second it will stick. Meanwhile he can hear snatches from time to time of what the men are saying; when they talk politics he always wants to be right among them, for they know nothing, he thinks, and need him to explain everything. But now he can't leave the cooking-pot, and gives little hops of desperation, wringing his hands; 'Capitalism!' he shouts now and again, 'Exploitation by the bourgeoisie,' as if suggesting ideas to the men, who refuse to listen to him.

'In Naples in '40,' explains Carabiniere, 'there was a great battle between students and Carabinieri! And if we Carabinieri had defeated them there wouldn't have been a war! But the students wanted to burn down the town hall! Mussolini was forced to make war!'

'Poor old Mussolini!' jeer the others.

'To hell with you and your Mussolini!' shouts Duke.

From the kitchen comes Mancino's voice, bleating: 'Mussolini! Imperialist bourgeoisie!'

'The town hall, they tried to burn the town hall! So what

could us Carabinieri do? If we'd put them in their places, though, Mussolini would never have started the war!'

Mancino, torn between his duty to the cooking-pot and his longing to go and talk about revolution, is bleating away until finally he attracts the attention of Long Zena and signals to him to come over. Long Zena thinks he is being called to taste the rice and decides to make the effort to get up. Mancino shouts: 'Imperialist bourgeoisie, tell 'em it's the bourgeoisie making war for its markets!'

'Oh, shit,' says Long Zena and turns his back on him. Mancino's speeches always bore him to death; he can't understand them, he knows nothing about the bourgeosie or communism, and he is not attracted by a world in which everyone has to work, he prefers one in which everyone is out for himself and is working as little as possible.

'Free enterprise,' yawns Long Zena, flopping down among the rhododendrons again, and scratching himself through the holes in his trousers, 'I'm for free enterprise; and everyone being free to get rich by his own efforts.'

Carabiniere is now explaining his conception of history; there are two forces struggling against each other, the Carabinieri, who are poor unfortunates trying to keep order, and the students, the big-shots, the *cavalieri*, the lawyers, doctors, *commendatori*, those with salaries undreamt of, even by the Carabinieri, and who still aren't satisfied and send the Carabinieri to fight the wars in order to get more.

'You don't understand anything!' shouts Mancino, who cannot hold out another moment and has now left Pin to look after the cooking-pot. 'Imperialism is caused by over-production!'

'Back to your cooking!' they shout at him. 'And make sure the rice doesn't stick this time too!'

But Mancino is now standing in the middle of them, his little body enveloped in the big sailor's jerkin with its shoulders covered with hawk's droppings, waving his fists in an endless speech about capitalist imperialism, arms traffic and the universal revolution that will take place when the war is over, in England and America too, and the abolition of frontiers by the International and the Red Flag.

The men lie sprawled among the rhododendrons their thin faces covered with matted beard, their hair all over their foreheads; they wear odd pieces of uniform, all tending in colour towards a dirty grey; firemen's or Fascist or German tunics with the badges torn off. All of them are there for different reasons – many are deserters from the Fascist forces or freed prisoners, some are still boys, impelled by an obstinate impulse, a vague longing to go against things.

They all dislike Mancino because he vents himself in words and arguments, not in shooting; to them his arguments seem useless, as he talks about enemies they know nothing about, such as capitalists and financiers. It's rather like Mussolini expecting the Italians to hate the British and the Abyssinians, whom none of them had ever seen, and who live beyond the ocean. And the men pull the cook in among them, play leap-fog over his little curved shoulders and hit him on his big bald head, while the hawk turns nasty and rolls its eyes.

Dritto, still a little way off, now intervenes, dangling his machine-gun against his knees. 'Go and see to the food, Mancino.'

Dritto does not like discussions much either; or rather he only likes to talk about actions and weapons, about the new small tommy-guns which the Fascists are beginning to use and how he would like to lay his hands on one; but what he likes more than anything is giving orders, getting the men into position under cover while he himself jumps up to fire short bursts.

'Go on, the rice is burning, can't you smell it?' shout the men at Mancino, pushing him away.

Mancino calls on the commissar for support: 'Hey, Giacinto, why don't you say something? What d'you think you're doing? They're right to call this the Fascist detachment, you can't even talk politics here!'

Giacinto has just returned from headquarters, but has not yet said if there is any news; all he has done is shrug his shoulders and mutter that the brigade commissar would be passing before nightfall on inspection. After hearing this the men throw themselves down among the rhododendrons once more; now the brigade commissar will soon be here to arrange everything, and it's useless to worry. Dritto also thinks it's useless to worry, the brigade commissar will tell him what his fate is to be; and he too stretches out again among the rhododendrons, though more apprehensively, tearing up little bits of shrub in his fingers.

Mancino is now complaining to Giacinto that no one in the detachment ever talks to the men about why they are partisans and what communism is. Giacinto has lice clustered thick on his hair-roots, and all over the hairs on the lower part of his stomach little white eggs are sticking to every single hair; Giacinto goes on cracking eggs and lice between his thumb-nails with a little click, in a gesture that has now become mechanical.

'Well,' he begins in a resigned voice as if he does not want to disappoint anyone, even Mancino, 'each of us knows why he's a partisan. I was a tinker and used to go round in the country and my cry could be heard a long way off and the women would come and bring their broken cooking-pots for me to mend. I used to go into their houses and joke with the maids and was sometimes given eggs and a glass of wine. I used to repair the pots in a field and there were always kids all around watching me. Now I can't go round the country any more because I'd be arrested; and then the bombing has messed everything up too. That's why we're partisans; so we can be tinkers again and so eggs and wine can be cheap, and so we can't be arrested any more and there'll be no more air raids. And then we want communism too. Communism means there won't be any more houses where the door's banged in your face, so you're forced to enter by the chicken run at night. Communism means going into a house and, even if they're having soup, being given soup even if you are a tinker; and if they're eating panettone at Christmas then they'll give you panettone. That's what communism means. For example: here we all are so full of lice that they almost drag us about in our sleep. Now I've just been to brigade headquarters and seen they have insect powder there. Then I said, "Fine communists you are, you don't send this to our detachment." So they said they'd send some. That's what communism means.'

The men have listened to him attentively and with approval; these are things anyone can understand. One of them who is smoking passes his cigarette to a comrade, and another who has to go on guard promises not to cut his turn short and to stay the whole hour before calling for his relief. They all begin discussing the insect powder which is to be sent to them, if it will kill the eggs as well as the lice or if it will only stun the insects so that an hour later they'll be biting more than ever.

No one would be talking about the war any more, if Cousin did not begin speaking: 'Say what you like but according to my way of looking at it the war was started by women.'

When Cousin gets started on his views of women he is even more boring than the cook; but at least he makes no attempt to persuade anyone and just seems to be complaining on his own.

'I was a soldier in Albania, Greece, France and North Africa,' he says, 'I was in the Alpini for eighty-three months. And in every country I always saw all the women waiting for the soldiers to come out of barracks, and the more lice-ridden and filthy we were the more they liked us. I let myself be persuaded once and all I got out of it was the clap; for three months I had to lean against the wall every time I wanted to piss. Now when you're in a distant country and seeing no other women but those, the only consolation is thinking of your own home and your own wife if you has one, or of a fiancée, and saying to yourself, anyway *she's* alright. Then you comes back and yes, sir, find the wife, while you were away, has been drawing her allowance and going to bed with all the men around.'

The others know that Cousin is telling his own story, that his wife went with everyone while he was away and had children whose fathers were unknown.

'Even that's not enough, though,' Cousin goes on, 'd'you realize why our men are always being caught by the Fascists? Because the place is full of women acting as spies, of wives denouncing their husbands; why, at this very moment all our women are sitting on the Fascists' knees cleaning their guns for them to come and kill us with.'

The others are beginning to have enough of this now, and shout at him to stop; it's one thing his being unlucky with his wife and her denouncing him to the Germans to get rid of him and forcing him to take to the woods, but that is no good reason to insult everyone else's women.

'You see,' Cousin goes on, 'a woman only has to arrive in a place and ... you get what I mean.'

Now the men don't contradict him because they understand what he is referring to and want to hear how far he'll go.

'... a woman has only to arrive in a place and some fool at once loses his head over her ...' says Cousin. Cousin is a man who likes being friendly with everyone, but he has a sharp tongue and when he has something to say he doesn't care who he says it to.

'. . . it doesn't matter when the fool is just anyone, but if he's a fool with responsibilities . . .'

The men look at Dritto; he's a little way off, but certainly listening. The men are a little afraid that Cousin may go too far and cause a terrific row.

'. . . and ends up by setting fire to a house because of a woman . . .'

There, he's said it, think the men, now something will happen. It's better this way, they say, someone had to say it some time.

But at that moment a roar is heard above them and the whole sky is filled with aeroplanes. All attention shifts to them. It is a big formation of bombers; soon some town will be left gutted and smoking beneath them, while they vanish into the clouds. Pin feels the earth vibrating under the roar and thinks of the tons of waiting bombs passing over his head. At that moment the Old Town must be emptying and people crowding into the muddy tunnel. From the south comes the deep sound of falling bombs.

Pin sees that Dritto has gone up on to a rise and is looking down into the valley through his binoculars. He joins him. Dritto is smiling his evil sad smile, as he turns the lenses.

'Can I have a look too, Dritto?' asks Pin.

'Here you are,' says Dritto, and passes him the binoculars.

Through a coloured confusion in the lenses gradually appears the crest of the last hills before the sea, and a big white cloud rising. More explosions can be heard down there; the bombing is still going on.

'Fine, destroy everything!' shouts Dritto, beating his fist against his palm. 'My own house first! Fling everything down! My own house first!'

CHAPTER NINE

Towards dusk arrive Ferriera and Kim, the commander and the commissar of the brigade. Mist is rising outside in wisps, like dust from a series of slammed doors, and in the barn the men crouch round the fire with the two from brigade headquarters. These hand round a packet of cigarettes until it is empty. They are men of few words. Ferriera is a sturdy young man, with an Alpine cap, a small blond beard, and a pair of big cold clear eyes with which he constantly glances up through half-closed lids. Kim is skinny, with a long reddish face, and moustaches which he is continually chewing.

Ferriera is a workman, born in the mountains, and is cold and clear by nature; he listens to everything with a slight smile of assent and has meanwhile already made up his mind on his own – how the brigade is to be deployed, where the machine-guns are to be placed, when the mortars should go into action. For him partisan warfare is as exact and precise as a machine; he has taken the revolutionary impulse matured in factories up into the mountains where he was born, and his courage and cunning is now used in places every yard of which he knows.

Kim, on the other hand, is a student; he has a great yearning for logic, for certainty about cause and effect, and yet his mind is apt to crowd at every second with unanswered questions. He has an enormous interest in humanity; that is why he is a medical student, for he knows that the explanation of everything is to be found in the grinding, moving cells of the human body, and not in philosophic speculation. He will become a mental specialist, a psychiatrist. The men do not like him very much because he looks them fixedly in the eyes as if he were trying to discover the source of their thoughts; and then he comes out suddenly with point-blank questions that have nothing to do with the conversation, about their childhood or love-life. For him also, behind human beings, there is the great machine of class progress, the machine that is fed by little daily gestures and in which other gestures burn away without leaving a trace; the machine of history. Everything must be logical, everything must be understood, both in history and in men's minds; but there is still a gap between one and the other, a dark area where collective motives become individual motives, forming monstrous deviations and unexpected combinations. And Kim goes round the detachments every day with his slim Sten-gun hanging from one shoulder, talking to the commissars and commanders, studying the men, analysing the position of each one, breaking every problem down into its component parts; 'a, b, c,' he says; everything must be clear, clear in others as it is to him.

Now the men are crowding round Ferriera and Kim, asking for news of the war; of that distant war on the military fronts, and of the threatening one nearby, their own. Ferriera explains that they should not expect any help from the Allied armies, he is convinced that the partisans will be able to cope with the enemy on their own. Then Ferriera tells them the great news of the day: a German column is advancing up the valley, to comb the entire mountain-range; they know where the partisan camps are and will burn houses and villages all around. But at dawn the whole brigade will move up on to the crest of the mountains, and will also be reinforced by other brigades; the Germans will suddenly find themselves exposed on the main road under a hail of fire and will be forced to retreat.

Then the men all break into movement; their backs ripple,

they clasp hands, jerk out words through clenched teeth; it's the battle already starting in them, their faces are already tensed and hardened into fighting expressions, their hands groping for weapons to feel the touch of steel.

'They saw the fire, that's why they're coming: we knew it,' says someone. Dritto is standing a little apart, the flickering flames lighting his lowered lids.

'The fire, yes, because of the fire too, of course. But there's another reason,' says Kim, slowly blowing out a mouthful of smoke; the men stand there silently; Dritto also raises his eyes.

'We've been betrayed by one of our own men,' says Kim. Then the atmosphere becomes tense, as if a wind were cutting into the men's bones; the wind of betrayal, cold and damp as a wind off the marshes, a wind which strikes them every time news like this reaches the partisan camp.

'Who was it?'

'Pelle. He went to the Black Brigade. Just like that, on his own, without being captured. Thanks to him four of our men who were in prison there have already been shot. He takes part in the interrogations of anyone caught and betrays them all.'

This is the kind of news that clogs the men's blood with despair, and prevents them thinking. Pelle was there with them, only a few nights before, saying: 'Listen, I'll tell you an action we can carry out!' It seems strange not to hear his wheezy breathing behind them as he greases a machine-gun for the next day's action. Instead of which Pelle is now down there in the forbidden town, wearing a big death's head on his black cap and carrying beautiful new weapons, no longer frightened of round-ups, and driven as always by that inner frenzy of his which makes him blink his cold-reddened eyes and lick his parched lips flecked with saliva, a frenzy now turned against his former comrades, but without hatred or rancour, as if he were playing a game with friends in which the stake is death.

Suddenly Pin thinks of his pistol; perhaps Pelle has found it, as he knows all the paths by the river-bed from taking girls there, and now he is wearing it oiled and gleaming all over, as his weapons usually are, on his Black Brigade uniform. Or perhaps he was just lying when he said he knew the place where the spiders make their nests, and had used the story as an excuse for going down into the town to betray his comrades and get issued with those new, almost silent German weapons.

'We must kill him now,' the men say to each other, as if they were accepting a necessity; perhaps, secretly, they would prefer to see him return next day, loaded up with new weapons, and continue his private war with and against them in that grim game of his.

'Red Wolf has gone down into the town to organize the *Gap* against him,' says Ferriera.

'I'll go too,' various men say. But Ferriera says that now they must concentrate on getting ready for next day's battle, which will be a decisive one. The men scatter to prepare their weapons and apportion jobs.

Ferriera and Kim call Dritto aside.

'We've had a report on the fire,' they say.

'It was just one of those things,' says Dritto. He has no desire to justify himself. Nothing matters now.

'Is there anyone else responsible for the fire?' asks Kim.

And Dritto says: 'It was all my fault.'

The two gaze seriously at him. Dritto is thinking how much he would like to leave the partisans and hide away in a place he knows of, till the end of the war.

'Have you any excuse to offer?' they ask him, with a patience that gets on his nerves.

'No. It was just one of those things.'

Now they'll either say: 'Leave' or 'We'll shoot you.' Instead of which Ferriera says: 'All right. We'll talk about this another day. Do you feel up to it, Dritto?'

Dritto's yellow eyes are on the ground. 'I'm ill,' he says.

'You must try to get really well for tomorrow,' says Kim. 'It's very important for you too, the battle tomorrow. Very, very important. Think it over.'

They do not take their eyes off him and Dritto feels a mounting longing to let himself drift.

'I'm ill,' he says, 'I'm very ill.'

'Now,' says Ferriera. 'Tomorrow you must keep along the crest of Mount Pellegrino from the pilon to the second gorge, d'you understand? There you'll get orders where to move to. Keep the squads well apart; the machine-guns are to go with the gunners and riflemen so that they can move together when necessary. Every single man must go into action, without any exception, even the quartermaster, even the cook.'

Dritto has followed all this with little nods of assent, and occasional shakes of his head.

'No exceptions,' he repeats, 'not even the cook?' and he listens attentively.

'You must all be up on the crest by dawn, d'you understand?' Kim looks at him, chewing his moustache. 'Are you quite sure you understand, Dritto?'

There almost seems a tone of affection in his voice, but perhaps it's just persuasion, as it's such an important battle.

'I'm very ill,' says Dritto, 'very ill.'

Kim and Ferriera are walking along the dark mountainside towards another encampment.

'Surely you see now it was a mistake, Kim?' says Ferriera.

Kim shakes his head. 'No, it's not a mistake,' he says.

'But it is,' says the commander, 'it was a mistaken idea of yours to make up a detachment entirely of men who can't be trusted, with a commander who can be trusted even less. You see what happens. If we'd divided them up among the good ones it might have kept them on the right lines.'

Kim continues to chew his moustache. 'For my part,' he says, 'this is the detachment I'm most pleased with.'

At this Ferriera nearly loses his calm; he raises his ice-cold eyes and rubs his forehead. 'But Kim, when will you realize that this is a fighting brigade, not an experimental laboratory? I can understand your getting a scientific satisfaction from watching the reactions of these men, all arranged as you wanted them, proletariat in one part, peasants in another, then "sub-proletariat", as you call it . . . The political work you ought to be doing, it seems to me, is mixing them all up together and giving class-consciousness to those who haven't got it, so as to achieve this blessed unity we hear so much about . . . Apart from the military value, of course . . .'

Kim, who has difficulty in expressing himself, shakes his head.

'Nonsense,' he says. 'Nonsense. The men all fight with the same sort of urge in them . . . well, not quite the same, . . . each has an urge of his own . . . but they're all fighting in unison now, each as much as the other. Then there's Dritto, there's Pelle . . . You don't understand what it costs them . . . Well, they too have the same urge . . . Any little thing is enough to save or lose them . . . That's what political work is . . . to give them a sense . . .'

When Kim talks to the men and analyses the situation for them, he is absolutely clear and dialectical. But when he is talking like this just for one other person to hear him, it makes one's head spin. Ferriera sees things more simply. 'All right, let's give them this sense, let's organize them the way I say.'

137

Kim breathes through his moustache. 'This isn't an army, you see, they aren't soldiers to whom one can say: this is your duty. You can't talk about duty here, you can't talk about ideals like country, liberty, communism. The men don't want to hear about ideals, anyone can have those, they have ideals on the other side too. You see what happens when that extremist cook begins his sermonizing? They shout at him and knock him about. They don't need ideals, myths, or to shout "Long live . . ." They fight and die without shouting anything.'

'Why do they fight, then?' asks Ferriera. He knows why he does, everything is perfectly clear to him.

'Well,' says Kim, 'at this moment the various detachments are climbing silently up towards their positions. Tomorrow many of them will be wounded or dead. They know that. What drives them to lead this life, what makes them fight? Well, first, the peasants who live in these mountains, it's easier for them. The Germans burn their villages, take away their cattle. Theirs is a basic human war, one to defend their own country, for the peasants really have a country. So they join up with us, young and old, with their old shot-guns and corduroy hunting-jackets; whole villages of them; they're with us as we're defending their country. And defending their country becomes a serious ideal for them, transcends them, as an end in itself; they sacrifice even their homes, even their cattle, to go on fighting. Then there are other peasants for whom "country" remains something selfish; *their* cattle, *their* homes, *their* crops. And to keep all that they become spies, Fascists . . . there are whole villages which are our enemies. Then there are the workers. The workers have a background of their own, of wages and strikes, work and struggle elbow to elbow. They're a class, the workers are. They know there's something better in life and they fight for that something better. They have a "country" too, a "country" still to be conquered, and they're fighting here to conquer it. Down in the town there are factories which will be theirs; they can already see the red writing on the factory walls and the banners flying on the factory chimneys. But there's no sentimentality in them. They understand reality and how to change it. Then there is an intellectual or a student or two, very few of them though, here and there, with ideas in their heads that are often vague or twisted. Their "country" consists of words, or at the most of some books. But as they fight they find that those words of theirs no longer have any meaning, and they make new discoveries about men's struggles, and they just fight on without asking themselves questions, until they find new words and rediscover the old ones, changed now, with unsuspected meanings. Who else is there? Foreign prisoners, who've escaped from concentration camps and joined us; they're fighting for a real proper country, a distant country which they want to get back to and which is theirs just because it is distant. But, after all, can't you see that this is only a struggle between symbols? that to kill a German, a man must think not of that German but of another German, with a substitution technique which is enough to turn his brain? that everything and everybody must become a Chinese shadow-play, a myth?'

Ferriera strokes his blond beard; he doesn't see any of these things.

'It's not like that,' he says.

'No, it's not like that,' Kim goes on, 'I know that too. It's not like that. Because there's something else, common to all of them: an inner frenzy. Take Dritto's detachment; petty thieves, *carabinieri*, ex-soldiers, black marketeers, down-and-outs; men on the fringes of society, who got along somehow despite all the chaos around them, with nothing to defend and

139

nothing to lose; either that, or they're defective physically, or they have fixations, or they're fanatics. No revolutionary idea can ever appear in them, tied as they are to the millstones grinding them. Or if it does it will be born twisted, the product of rage and humiliation, like that cook's extremism. Why do they fight, then? They have no "country", either real or invented. And yet you know there's courage, there's a frenzy in them too. It comes from the squalor of their streets, the filth of their homes, the obscenities they've known ever since childhood, the strain of having to be bad. And any little thing, a false step, a momentary impulse, is enough to send them over to the other side, to the Black Brigade, like Pelle, there to shoot with the same frenzy, the same hatred, against either side, it doesn't matter which.'

Ferriera mutters into his beard: 'So you think the spirit of our men ... and the Black Brigade's ... the same thing?'

'The same thing, the same thing ... but, if you see what I mean ...' Kim has stopped, with a finger pointing as if he were keeping the place in a book, 'The same thing but the other way round. Because here we're in the right, there they're in the wrong. Here we're achieving something, there they're just reinforcing their chains. That age-old resentment which weighs down on Dritto's men, on all of us, including you and me, and which finds expression in shooting and killing enemies, the Fascists have that too: it forces them to kill with the same hope of purification and of release. But then there is also the question of history. The fact is that on our side nothing is lost, not a single gesture, not a shot, though each may be the same as theirs – d'you see what I mean? – they will all serve if not to free us then to free our children, to create a world that is serene, without resentment, a world in which no one has to be bad. The others are on the side of lost gestures, of useless resentment, which are lost and useless even if they

140

should win, because they are not making positive history, they are not helping to free themselves but to repeat and perpetuate resentment and hatred, until in another twenty or a hundred or a thousand years it will begin all over again, the struggle between us and them; and we shall both be fighting with the same anonymous hatred in our eyes, though always, perhaps without knowing it, *we* shall be fighting for redemption, *they* to remain slaves. That is the real meaning of the struggle now, the real, absolute meaning, beyond the various official meanings. An elementary, anonymous urge to free us from all our humiliations; the worker from his exploitation, the peasant from his ignorance, the petty bourgeois from his inhibitions, the outcast from his corruption. This is what I believe our political work is, to use human misery against itself, for our own redemption, as the Fascists use misery to perpetuate misery and man fighting man.'

Only the blue of Ferriera's eyes and the yellow glimmer of his beard can be seen in the dark. He shakes his head. He does not feel this resentment; he is precise as a mechanic and practical as a mountain-peasant; for him the struggle is a precise machine of which he knows the workings and purpose.

'It seems impossible,' he says, 'it seems impossible that with all that balls in your head you can still be a good commissar and talk clearly to the men.'

Kim is not displeased at Ferriera not understanding him; men like Ferriera must be talked to in exact terms; 'a, b, c,' one must say, things are either definite or they're 'balls', for them there are no ambiguous or dark areas. But Kim does not reason that way because he believes himself to be superior to Ferriera; no, his aim is to be able to think like Ferriera, to see no other reality but Ferriera's, nothing else matters.

'Well, I'll say good-bye.' They have reached a parting in the path. Now Ferriera will go on to Gamba's detachment and Kim to Baleno's. They have to separate in order to be able to inspect every detachment that night, before the battle.

Nothing else matters. Kim walks on alone, the slim Sten-gun hanging from his shoulder like a broken walking-stick. Nothing else matters. The tree trunks in the dark take on strange human shapes. Man carries his childhood fears with him for his whole life long. 'Perhaps,' thinks Kim, 'I'd be frightened, if I wasn't brigade commissar. Not to be frightened any more, that's the final aim of man.'

Kim is logical when he is analysing the situation with the detachment commissars, but when he is walking along alone and reasoning with himself things become mysterious and magical again, and life seems full of miracles. Our heads are still full of magic and miracles, thinks Kim. Sometimes he feels he is walking amid a world of symbols, like his namesake, little Kim in the middle of India, in that book of Kipling's which he had so often reread as a boy.

'Kim . . . Kim . . . Who is Kim . . . ?'

Why is he walking over the mountains that night, getting ready for a battle, with power over life and death, after that gloomy childhood of his as a rich man's son, and his shy adolescence? At times he feels at the mercy of crazy swings of mood, as if he's acting hysterically, but no, his thoughts are logical, he can analyse everything with perfect clarity. And yet, he's not serene. His parents were serene, those parents from the great middle class which created their own riches. The proletariat is serene for it knows what it wants, so are the peasants who are now doing sentry duty over their own villages. The Soviets are serene, they have made their minds up about everything and are now fighting with both passion and method, not because war is a fine thing but because it is necessary. The Bolsheviks! The Soviet Union is perhaps already a serene country, perhaps there is no more poverty there. Will Kim ever be serene? One day perhaps, we will all achieve serenity and will not understand so much because we will have understood everything.

Here men still have troubled eyes and haggard faces. Kim has become fond of these men, though. That little boy in Dritto's detachment, for instance. What's his name? With that rage eating up his freckly face, even when he laughs . . . He's said to be the brother of a prostitute. Why is he fighting? He doesn't know it's so that he should no longer be the brother of a prostitute. And those Calabrian brothers-in-law. They're fighting so as not to be despised folk from the south any more, poor immigrants, looked down on as foreigners in their own country. And that Carabiniere is fighting so that he won't feel a Carabiniere any more, always spying on his fellow man. Then there's Cousin, the good, gigantic, ruthless Cousin . . . They say he's out for revenge on a woman who betrayed him . . . We all have a secret wound which we are fighting to avenge. Even Ferriera? Yes, perhaps even Ferriera; the frustration of not being able to get the world to go as he wants it. Not Red Wolf, though. Because everything that Red Wolf wants is possible. He must be made to want the right thing, that is political work, commissar's work. And learn that what he wants is right; that too is political work, commissar's work.

Perhaps, one day, thinks Kim, I won't understand these things any more. I'll be serene, and understand men in a completely different way, a juster way, perhaps. Why perhaps? Well, I shan't say 'perhaps' any more then, there won't be any more 'perhaps' in me. And I'll have Dritto shot. Now I'm too linked to them and all their twists. To Dritto too. I know that Dritto must suffer a lot for always being determined to behave badly. Nothing in the world hurts so much as behaving badly. One day as a child I shut myself up for two days in my room

143

without eating. I suffered terribly but would not open the door and they had to come and fetch me by ladder through the window. I longed to be consoled and understood. Dritto is doing the same. But he knows we'll shoot him. He wants to be shot. That longing gets hold of men sometimes. And Pelle, what is Pelle doing at this moment?

Kim walks on through a larch wood and thinks of Pelle down in the town going round on curfew patrol with the death's head badge on his cap. Pelle must be alone, alone with his anonymous mistaken hatred, alone with his betrayal gnawing at him and making him behave worse than ever to justify it. He'll shoot at the cats in the black-out, even, from rage, and the shots will wake the bourgeoisie nearby, and make them start up in their beds.

Kim thinks of the column of Germans and Fascists who are perhaps at that moment advancing up the valley, towards the dawn which will bring death pouring down on their heads from the crests of the mountains. It is the column of lost gestures. One of the soldiers, waking up at a jolt of the truck is now thinking 'I love you, Kate.' In six or seven hours he'll be dead, we'll have killed him; even if he hadn't thought 'I love you, Kate,' it would have been the same; everything that he does or thinks is lost, cancelled from history.

I, on the other hand, am walking through a larch wood and every step I take is history. I think 'I love you, Adriana' and that is history, will have great consequences. I'll behave tomorrow in battle like a man who has thought tonight 'I love you, Adriana.' Perhaps I may not accomplish great deeds but history is made up of little anonymous gestures; I may die tomorrow even before that German, but everything I do before dying and my death too will be little parts of history, and all the thoughts I'm having now will influence my history tomorrow, tomorrow's history of the human race.

Now, instead of escaping into fantasy as I did when I was a child, I could be making a mental study of the details of the attack, the dispositions of weapons and squads. But I am too fond of thinking about those men, studying them, making discoveries about them. What will they do 'afterwards' for instance? Will they recognize in post-war Italy something made by them? Will they understand what system will have to be used then in order to continue our struggle, the long and constantly changing struggle to better humanity? Red Wolf will understand, I think; I wonder how he'll manage to put his understanding into practice, how will he use that adventurous, ingenious spirit of his when there are no more daring deeds or escapes to be made? They should all be like Red Wolf. We should all be like Red Wolf. There'll be some, on the other hand, whose anonymous resentment will continue, who will become individualists again, and thus sterile; they'll fall into crime, the great outlet for dumb resentments; they'll forget that history once walked by their side, breathed through their clenched teeth. The ex-Fascists will say: 'Oh, the partisans! I told you so! I realized it at once!' And they won't have realized anything, either before or after.

One day Kim will be serene. Everything is clear with him now. Dritto, Pin, the Calabrian brothers-in-law. He knows how to behave towards each of them, without fear or pity. Sometimes when he is walking at night the mists of souls seem to condense around him like the mists in the air; but he is a man who analyses; 'a, b, c,' he'll say to the commissars; he's a Bolshevik, a man who dominates situations. 'I love you, Adriana.'

The valley is full of mist, and Kim is walking along a slope which is as stony as a lakeside. The larches appear out of the mist like mooring-poles. *Kim ... Kim ... Who is Kim?* He feels like the hero of that novel read in his childhood; the half-English half-Indian boy who travels across India with the old Red Lama looking for the river of purification.

Two hours ago he was talking to that liar Dritto, to the prostitute's brother, and now he is reaching Baleno's detachment, the best in the brigade. There is a squad of Russians with Baleno, ex-prisoners who had escaped from the fortification works on the border.

'Who goes there?'

It's the sentry; a Russian.

Kim gives his name.

'Bring news, Commissar?'

It's Aleksjéi, the son of a moujik, an engineering student.

'Tomorrow there will be a battle, Aleksjéi.'

'Battle? Hundred Fascists *kaput*?'

'I don't know how many *kaput*, Aleksjéi. I don't even know how many alive.'

'*Sale e tabacchi*, Commissar.'

Sale e tabacchi, is the Italian phrase which has made most impression on Aleksjéi, he repeats it all the time, like a refrain, a talisman.

'*Sale e tabacchi*, Aleksjéi.'

Tomorrow there will be a big battle. Kim is serene. 'A, b, c,' he'll say. Again and again he thinks: 'I love you, Adriana.' That, and that alone, is history.

CHAPTER TEN

In the dark morning, without a glimmer of light, Dritto's men are moving silently around the barn, preparing to leave. They wrap blankets round their shoulders; it will be cold up on the boulders of the crest before dawn. As they do so they think not of what will happen to themselves but to the blanket that each takes with them. Will they lose it running away, will it be soaked with their blood as they lie dying, or be taken from them by a Fascist and shown round the town as booty? But what does a blanket matter?

Above them, as if the sound came from above the clouds, they can hear the enemy column on the move; big wheels turning on dusty roads without headlights, the tramp of tired men asking their section leader if they still have far to go. Dritto's men talk in whispers as if the column were passing right behind the walls of the barn.

Now they are spooning boiled chestnuts out of their billy-cans; no one knows when they will eat next. Even the cook will be going into action this time; he is ladling out the chestnuts, cursing under his breath, his eyes swollen with sleep. Giglia has also got up and is wandering round among the men's preparations without finding anything useful to do. Every now and again Mancino pauses to glance at her.

'Hey, Giglia,' he says, 'it's not safe for you to stay here in the camp alone. You never know.'

'Where d'you expect me to go to, then?' asks Giglia.

'Put on your skirt and go to a village, they won't do anything to a woman. Dritto, tell her to leave, she can't stay here alone.'

Dritto has not eaten any chestnuts, he is directing the men's preparations almost silently, with his collar up. He does not raise his head or reply at once.

'No,' he says eventually, 'she'd better stay here.'

Giglia glances at her husband as if to say, 'You see?' and ends up bumping into Cousin who, without even looking at her, snaps, 'Out of the way.' She turns on her heel, and goes back into the hut to sleep.

Pin is also in everybody's way, like a hunting dog watching its master's preparations.

'The battle,' he thinks, trying to excite himself, 'now there'll be the battle.'

'Well,' he says to Giacinto, 'which shall I take?'

The commissar takes no notice of him. 'What?' he says.

'Which rifle shall I take?' asks Pin.

'You?' exclaims Giacinto. 'You're not coming.'

'Yes, I am.'

'Out of the way. This isn't a time to take children along. Dritto doesn't want you to come. Out of the way.'

Pin is furious, he'll follow behind them unarmed, jeering at their backs till they turn and shoot at him.

'Dritto, Dritto, is it true you don't want me to come?'

Dritto doesn't reply, he is taking little puffs at a cigarette-end, as if he were biting it.

'There,' says Pin, 'stuff you lot, he says it's not true.'

Now I'll get a clip on the back of the head, he thinks. But Dritto says nothing.

'Can I go into action, Dritto?' says Pin.

Dritto smokes.

'Dritto says I can come, did you hear, Giacinto?' exclaims Pin.

Now Dritto will say: 'Shut up; you stay here.'

Instead of which he says nothing. Why?

Pin says, very loudly, 'Right, then I'm coming.'

And he goes slowly towards the place where there are still some unallotted weapons, whistling so as to attract attention to himself. He chooses the lightest rifle.

'Then I'll take this,' he says, loudly.

'Does it belong to anyone, this one?'

No answer. Pin goes back to where he was before, swinging the rifle to and fro by its strap. He sits down on the ground, right in front of Dritto, and begins testing the bolt, the firing-pin, the trigger, crooning: 'I've got a rifle! I've got a rifle!'

Someone shouts: 'Quiet! Are you mad?'

The men are getting into single file, squad by squad, group by group; the ammunition bearers arrange their shifts.

'You understand, then,' says Dritto, 'the detachment will take up position between the pilon on Mount Pellegrino and the second gorge. Cousin will take over command. You'll get new orders from the battalion when you arrive up there.'

Now all the men's eyes are on him, sleepy brooding eyes, crossed by locks of hair.

'What about you?' they ask.

Dritto's lowered eyelashes are covered with a slight discharge.

'I'm ill,' he says, 'I can't come.'

There, now they can say what they like. The men say nothing. 'I'm a finished man,' thinks Dritto. Now everything can take its course. It's terrible, though, that the men say nothing, make no protest; that means they've already condemned him, are pleased at his shirking this last test. Perhaps they expected it. And yet they cannot understand what it is that makes him do this; neither does he, Dritto, himself. But now everything can take its course, there is nothing for him to do but let himself drift.

Pin, on the other hand, understands everything; he is watching attentively, his tongue between his teeth, his cheeks burning. There lies the woman, with that warm breast of hers under the man's shirt, half-buried in the hay. She feels hot in the hay at night and she keeps on turning over. Once, she got up when everyone was asleep, took off her trousers and got back naked between the blankets. Pin saw her. Yes, while the battle rages in the valley astounding things will be happening in the barn,

149

things a hundred times more exciting. That must be why Dritto is allowing Pin to go into action. Pin has dropped the rifle at his feet and is following every movement with his eyes, very attentively. The men continue getting into line; no one tells Pin to do so.

At that moment the hawk begins screeching from the rafters in the roof, flapping its clipped wings as if in sudden desperation.

'Babeuf! I must feed Babeuf!' cries Mancino, and he runs to fetch the sack of entrails. Then the men turn against him and the bird, as if wanting to divert all their rancour on to something specific.

'Damn you and your hawk! Filthy bird of ill omen! Some disaster happens every time it opens its mouth! Twist its neck! Twist its neck!'

Mancino faces them with the hawk perched by the claws on his shoulder, feeding it bits of meat and looking at his comrades with hatred. 'The hawk's mine, it's nothing to do with you, and I'll take it into action with me if I want to, d'you get that?'

'Twist its neck!' cries Long Zena. 'This isn't the time to think of hawks! Twist its neck or we will!'

He tries to grab it, and gets a bite on the back of his hand that draws blood. The hawk's feathers are standing on end, it is spreading its wings and screeching ceaselessly, rolling its yellow eyes.

'There! There! I'm glad!' cries the cook. The men are all standing round him, their beards bristling with rage, their fists raised.

'Shut it up! Shut it up! It brings bad luck! It'll call the Germans down on us!'

Long Zena sucks the blood on his wounded hand.

'Kill it!' he shouts.

Duke, who is carrying the machine-gun, takes a pistol from his belt.

'I'll shoot it! I'll shoot it!' he grunts.

The hawk, rather than showing any sign of quietening down, is becoming more and more frenzied.

'Alright,' Mancino suddenly decides. 'Alright. Just see what I'm going to do. You wanted it.'

He has taken the hawk by the neck in both his hands and is now twisting it, holding the head between his knees, towards the ground. The men are all silent.

'There. Now you're satisfied. You're all satisfied, now. There.'

The hawk is not moving any more, its clipped wings are hanging open, its stiff feathers drooping. Mancino flings it on to a bush, and Babeuf remains hanging there by its wings, with its head down. It gives a last quiver, then dies.

'Into line. All into line and let's go,' calls Cousin. 'Machine-gunners ahead, ammunition bearers behind. Riflemen last. Let's go.'

Pin is standing to one side. He does not get into line. Dritto turns and enters the barn. In silence the men start off along the track leading up into the mountains. Last is Mancino in his sailor's jerkin with the bird-droppings all over his shoulders.

Inside the barn the darkness smells of hay. The woman and the man are asleep in opposite corners, wrapped in their blankets. Neither moves. Pin could swear, though, that neither will close an eye again till daybreak. He lies down also, with his eyes open. He will look and listen, and not close an eye either. The two are not even scratching themselves. They are breathing deeply. Yet they are awake, Pin knows that; and gradually he falls asleep.

It is daylight outside when he wakes up. Pin is all alone among trampled straw. Gradually he remembers everything.

It's the day of the battle! Why is there no sound of firing? It's the day when the commander will have the cook's wife! Pin gets up and goes out. The sky is so blue it's almost frightening, and so many birds singing they're almost frightening too.

The kitchen has been set up among the ruins of an old hut. Giglia is inside. She is fanning a small fire under a can full of chestnuts; she looks pale, with dull eyes.

'Pin! D'you want some chestnuts?' she calls with that false motherly air of hers as if she were trying to keep him sweet.

Pin hates women putting on maternal airs; he knows it's all a trick and that they, like his sister, really hate him and are just afraid of him. He hates her.

Has 'it' happened? And where is Dritto? He decides to ask her.

'Well; done everything?' he asks.

'What?' exclaims Giglia.

Pin does not reply; he glances at her from half-closed eyes, wrinkling his nose.

'I've just got up,' says Giglia, looking angelic.

She knows what I mean – thinks Pin – the cow. She's understood.

And yet he has a feeling that nothing definite has happened yet; the woman is looking tense and holding her breath.

Dritto arrives. He's been washing; around his neck is a faded coloured towel. His face looks older, covered with lines and shadows.

'They're not firing yet,' he says.

'Hell, Dritto,' exclaims Pin. 'Have they all fallen asleep?'

Dritto doesn't smile; he is sucking his teeth.

'Has the whole brigade fallen asleep on the crest, d'you think?' says Pin. 'And the Germans getting here on tiptoe? *Raus! Raus!* We turn round and there they are.'

Pin points behind Dritto, who turns around. Then he is

annoyed with himself for turning, and shrugs his shoulders. He sits down by the fire.

'I'm ill,' he says.

'D'you want some chestnuts?' asks Giglia.

Dritto spits into the cinders.

'No, they give me indigestion,' he says.

'Just drink the juice.'

'That does the same.'

Then he thinks it over. 'Alright. Give me some,' he says.

He brings the lip of the dirty billy-can to his lips and drinks. Then he puts it down.

'Good. I'm eating too,' says Pin.

And he begins to spoon up the mess of hot chestnuts.

Dritto raises his eyes towards Giglia. His eyelids have long hard lashes on top; the ones underneath are bare.

'Dritto,' says the woman.

'Mmm.'

'Why didn't you go?'

Pin keeps his face inside the tin and looks at them from above the brim.

'Go where?'

'Into action, of course.'

'How can I go anywhere, when I don't know where I am myself!'

'What's wrong, Dritto?'

'What's wrong? I know what's wrong! They've got it in for me at brigade headquarters, they've been playing cat and mouse with me for some time. It's always: hey, Dritto we'll talk about this afterwards, now listen, Dritto, think it over, Dritto watch out, this is the final push . . . To hell with all this . . . Devil take them. I can't stand it any more. If they've something to say to me let them say it. I want to do what I want, for a change.'

Giglia is sitting a little above him. She gives him a long look, breathing hard through her nostrils.

'I feel I want to do what I want, for a change,' Dritto tells her, his eyes yellow. He puts a hand on her knee.

Pin is sucking noisily at the empty tin.

'Dritto, suppose they really get at you?'

Dritto moves nearer her, now he is crouching at her feet.

'I don't mind dying,' he says. But his lips are trembling, the lips of a sick boy. 'I don't mind dying. But first I'd like ... First ...'

His head is turned up and he is looking at Giglia above him.

Pin throws the empty tin on to the ground, with the spoon inside. Ding! goes the spoon.

Dritto now turns his head towards him, and looks at him, gnawing his lips.

'Eh?' says Pin.

Dritto gives a start.

'They're not firing,' he says.

'They're not firing,' says Pin.

Dritto gets up, and walks round a little, nervously.

'Go and fetch some water, Pin.'

'Right away,' says Pin, and bends down to do up his boots.

'You're pale, Giglia,' says Dritto. He is standing behind her, with his knees touching her back.

'Perhaps I'm ill too,' breathes Giglia.

Pin breaks out into one of his monotonous songs in an endless crescendo: 'She's pale! ... She's pale! ... She's pale! ... She's pale! ...'

The man has put his hands on her cheeks and turned her face up. 'Ill like me ... ? Tell me, Giglia, ill like me ... ?'

'She's pale! ... She's pale! ... She's pale! ...' sings Pin.

Dritto turns on him with a furious face.

'Will you go and get me that water?'

'Wait a sec . . .' says Pin. 'I'll just do the other up.'

And he goes on fiddling with his boots.

'I don't know how you're ill . . .' says Giglia. 'How are you ill?'

Dritto says in a low voice, 'So ill I can't stand it any more, can't stand it any more.'

Now, still from behind her, he has taken her by the shoulders and is holding his hands under her arm-pits.

'She's pale! . . . She's pale! . . .'

'Pin!'

'Right. I'm off now. Give me the flask.'

Then he stops, with a hand to his ear. Dritto also stops, and looks out into the emptiness.

'They're not firing,' he says.

'Neh? They're not firing at all . . .' says Pin.

They both stand there silently.

'Pin!'

'I'm going!'

Pin leaves, dangling the flask and whistling the tune he has been singing. There'll be a lot to amuse him today. Pin will be quite pitiless; Dritto does not frighten him now he's not in command any more; he'll never command anything again, now he's refused to go into action. Pin's whistling can no longer be heard from the kitchen. He stops, turns round and tiptoes back. Will they already be on top of each other on the ground, biting each other's necks like dogs? Pin is already back in the kitchen, in the ruined hut. No, they're still where they were. Dritto's hands are now under her hair, at the nape of her neck, and she is making cat-like movements as if to avoid them. They turn at once, with a start, sensing his presence.

'Well?' exclaims Dritto.

155

'I came to fetch the other flask,' says Pin. 'The straw's undone on this one.'

Dritto runs a hand over his forehead. 'Here you are.'

The woman gets up and goes and sits near the sack of potatoes.

'Well. Let's peel some potatoes; at least we'll be doing something.'

She lays an empty sack on the ground and puts potatoes and a couple of knives on it.

'Take a knife, Dritto, here are the potatoes,' she says.

Pin thinks her silly and hypocritical.

Dritto is still running his hand over his forehead. 'They're not firing yet,' he says, 'I wonder what's happening?'

Pin goes out again; this time he really will go and fetch water. They'll have to be given time, otherwise nothing will ever happen. Near the spring is a bush laden with blackberries. Pin settles down to picking and eating them. He likes blackberries, but finds they give him no pleasure now; although he fills his mouth with them he can't taste any flavour. There; now he's eaten enough, he can return. But perhaps it's still too soon; better if he can get something else over first. He crouches down among the bushes. It makes him feel good to force himself and meanwhile think of Dritto and Giglia chasing each other round the ruined hut, or of those prisoners being led out into the darkness, naked and yellow, and made to kneel down in the graves they've dug themselves, with chattering teeth; evil incomprehensible things, as strangely fascinating to him as his own excrement.

He wipes himself with leaves. He's ready, off he goes.

In the kitchen the potatoes are spilled all over the floor. Giglia is in a corner beyond the sacks and cooking-pots, with a knife in her hand. Her man's shirt is open: inside it are her warm white breasts! Dritto is also standing on the other side of

156

the sacks, and is threatening her with his knife. Yes, they are chasing each other, perhaps they'll wound each other next!

Instead of which, he is laughing; they are both laughing; it's all a game. It's not nice laughter, and the joke seems to hurt them, but they are laughing.

Pin puts down the flask. 'Water,' he says loudly.

They leave their knives now and come to drink. Dritto takes the flask and gives it to Giglia. Giglia grasps it and drinks, while Dritto looks at her lips.

He says, 'They're not firing yet.'

Then he turns towards Pin. 'They're not firing yet,' he repeats. 'What on earth's happening down there?'

Pin is pleased at being asked a question like that, as if they were equals.

'What d'you think can be happening?' he asks.

Dritto drinks in great gulps, empties the flask down his throat, as if he's never going to stop. He dries his mouth. 'There, Giglia, if you want any more. Drink up if you're thirsty, then we'll send for another.'

'If you want me to,' says Pin sourly, 'I'll bring you a pailful.'

They both look at each other and laugh. But Pin realizes they're not laughing at what he said; it's a laugh between the two of them, secret, without any reason.

'If you like,' says Pin, 'I'll bring you enough to bathe in.'

They go on looking at each other and laughing.

'To bathe in,' repeats the man, and it's difficult now to tell if he's laughing or if his teeth are chattering. 'To bathe in, Giglia, to bathe in.'

He has taken her by the shoulders. Then suddenly his face darkens and he drops his hands. 'Down there,' he says, 'look down there.'

157

Hanging on a bush, a few yards away, is the dead hawk, dangling on its wings.

'Away with it. Away with the filthy thing,' he says, 'I don't want to see it any more!'

He takes it up by one of its wings and flings it far into the rhododendrons; Babeuf flies off as perhaps he never did in his life. Giglia puts a hand on Dritto's arm. 'No, poor Babeuf!'

'Away with it,' Dritto is pale with anger. 'I don't want to see it any more! Go and bury it, Pin! Pin, go and bury it. Take the spade and bury it, Pin!'

Pin looks at the dead bird in the rhododendrons; suppose it gets up, dead though it is, and bites him right between the eyes?

'No, I won't,' he says.

Dritto's nostrils quiver; he puts a hand on his pistol.

'Take the spade, Pin, and get going.'

Pin takes the hawk up by a leg; the claws are curved, and hard like hooks. He sets off with the spade on his shoulders, carrying the dead bird with its head dangling down. Through the rhododendrons and a patch of woodland and he's out in the meadows. Under those meadows rising in gradual slopes up towards the mountains all the dead are buried, with eyes full of earth, dead enemies and dead comrades. And now the hawk as well.

Pin walks over the meadows in curious twists and turns. He doesn't want, when he digs a grave for the bird, to uncover a human face with his spade. He doesn't want to disturb the dead at all, he's afraid of them. And yet it would be fine to dig up a dead body, a naked corpse with his teeth bare and his eyes empty.

Now Pin can only see mountains around him, and huge valleys with invisible depths, and high rocky slopes black with woods, then mountains again, row after row of them, into the infinite distance. He is alone on the earth. Under the earth are the dead. Beyond the woods and slopes is the rest of humanity, males and females rubbing themselves against each other on the ground, others attacking and killing. At his feet lies the dead hawk. Huge clouds are flying above him in the windswept sky. Pin begins digging out a grave for the dead bird. A small grave is enough; a hawk is not a man. Pin takes it up; its eyes are shut, with bare, white, almost human-looking lids. If he tried to open one, he would see the round yellow eye beneath. He feels an impulse to fling the hawk into the great empty space above the valley and see its wings open, then watch it rise in flight, circle above his head and fly off towards a distant peak. And then he would follow it as they do in fairy stories, walking over mountains and plains until he reached an enchanted land where all the inhabitants were good. But instead Pin now puts the hawk down into the grave and rakes earth on it with the tip of the spade.

At that moment an explosion like a thunderbolt fills the valley; shots, bursts, deep bangs, all amplified by echoes. The battle! Pin jumps back in terror. Terrible noises lacerate the air very near him, he can't tell where. Soon bullets will be falling right on top of him. Soon the Germans will be appearing on the rocky slopes, bristling with machine-guns, and be on him.

'Dritto!'

Pin runs away. He's left the spade sticking in the earth of the grave. He runs with the lacerating noises exploding all round him.

'Dritto! Giglia!'

There; now he's tearing through the wood. Machine-gun fire, grenades, mortars; the battle has suddenly started out of its sleep and it's impossible to tell where it is; perhaps only a few yards from him; perhaps he'll see machine-guns firing at him at the turn of this path, and dead men lying among the bushes.

'Help! Dritto! Giglia!'

He is out among the rhododendrons now. Under the open sky the shooting is more frightening than ever.

'Dritto! Giglia!'

No one in the kitchen. They've escaped! Left him alone!

'Dritto! They're firing! They're firing!'

Pin runs haphazardly among the banks of rhododendrons, sobbing. There, in the bushes, is a blanket, a blanket wrapped round a moving human body; one body . . . no, two bodies . . . two pairs of legs are showing . . . twined together . . . heaving up and down.

'The battle! Dritto! They're firing! The battle!'

CHAPTER ELEVEN

The brigade has reached the Pass of the Half-Moon after endless hours of marching. There is a cold night wind blowing which freezes the sweat into the bones; the men are too tired to sleep and the commanders order a short halt behind some rocky boulders. In the dim, cloudy darkness the pass looks like a concave bowl with its rims wreathed in mist, from which rise the top of two rocky heights. Beyond it lie free plains and valleys, fresh areas not yet occupied by the enemy. The men have not rested since they set off for the battle, yet they show no sign of any of those dangerous collapses of morale which are apt to come suddenly after long strain; the stimulant of battle has not worn off yet.

The battle has been a bloody one and ended in retreat; but

it was not lost. The Germans, passing through a defile, had suddenly found the heights around pullulating with shouting men and blazing with firearms; many of them had rolled into the ditches at the side of the road, one or two lorries began belching fire and smoke like furnaces and were soon reduced to nothing but black scrap-iron. Reinforcements then came up, but there was little they could do except wipe out a few partisans who had stayed on the road against orders or been cut off in the confusion. For the partisan commanders had been warned in time of the new motorized column approaching, and to avoid being surrounded had withdrawn their men up the mountain paths. The Germans, however, are not people to be put off by a reverse, and Ferriera has decided that the entire brigade is to evacuate the area, which could now become a trap, and move on into other valleys which could be more easily defended. Now the blackness of the night was left behind as the retreating men wound up, silent and orderly, along a mule path leading to the pass; in the rear came a line of mules carrying rations and ammunition, and the wounded from the battle.

Dritto's men are now chattering with cold behind the boulders; their heads and shoulders are wrapped in blankets, like Arab burnouses. The detachment has had one casualty – the commissar, Giacinto the tinker. He had been hit by a burst of German fire and his body lay in a meadow below, rid now of all his colourful dreams of vagabondage and of all his lice too, which no insect powder had ever done. There was also one man slightly wounded in a hand, Count, one of the Calabrian brothers-in-law.

They have now been joined by Dritto, whose yellow face and blanket round his shoulders make him look really ill. Silent, his nostrils quivering, he watches the men one by one. Every now and again he seems on the point of giving some order, then says

161

nothing. The men have not said a word to him yet. If he gave an order, or any of them talked to him, the rest would certainly turn on him, and violent words would fly. But this is not the moment for a show-down; both he and the men realize that by tacit consent, so he avoids giving orders or reprimands and the men avoid any occasion for them. The detachment has been marching with discipline, and there has been no dispersion or quarrel about shifts; one could never have told it was leaderless. But Dritto is still in fact their leader, he only has to glance at a man to make him straighten up; yes, he is a great leader, he has a magnificent leader's temperament, Dritto.

Pin, wrapped up to the eyes in a woollen scarf, is looking at Dritto and Giglia, and from them to Mancino. Their faces seem quite normal, perhaps rather drawn from cold and exhaustion; there is nothing on any of their faces to show what part they had played in the events of the morning before.

Other detachments pass which are to halt farther on or continue their march.

'Gian! Gian!'

In a squad which has halted nearby, Pin suddenly recognizes his old friend from the tavern, Gian the driver, dressed as a partisan and armed from head to foot. At first he does not realize who is calling him, then he is just as surprised himself: 'Oh . . . Pin!'

They greet each other with rather cautious warmth, as people do who are not used to exchanging compliments. Gian looks a different man; he has only been with the partisans a week, and his eyes have already lost that look of a cave-dwelling animal, due to smoke and alcohol, which those of the men in the tavern have. He seems to want to let his beard grow all over his face. He is in Spada's detachment.

'When I joined the brigade Kim wanted to put me in your detachment . . .' says Gian. Pin thinks: He doesn't realize what that means, perhaps the man from the committee that night at the tavern reported badly on all of them.

'Hell, Gian, I wish we were together!' says Pin. 'Why didn't they put you with us?'

'They told me it was pointless; your detachment is to be broken up soon!'

There, thinks Pin, he's only just arrived and knows all the latest news about us. Pin, on the other hand, knows nothing about things down in the town. 'Gian!' he says, 'what's the news from Long Alley? And the tavern?'

Gian looks at him sourly: 'Haven't you heard?' he asks.

'No,' says Pin, 'what is it? Has the Bersagliera had a child?'

Gian spits. 'I don't want to hear another word about those people,' he says. 'I'm ashamed of being born among them. For years I've been fed up to my teeth with them and the tavern, the stink of piss in the alley . . . And yet I stayed there . . . Now I've been forced to run away I can almost thank the swine who informed on me . . .'

'Michel the Frenchman?' asks Pin.

'Michel was one. But he's not the one who did most. He plays a double game, Michel does, with the Black Brigade and with the *Gap*; he hasn't properly decided yet which side to be on. . . .'

'And the others . . . ?'

'There was a round-up. They were all taken. We'd only just decided to form a *Gap* . . . Giraffe was shot . . . The others taken to Germany . . . The alley's almost emptied . . . A bomb from an aeroplane fell near the bakery; everyone has either evacuated or is living in the tunnel . . . It's another life here; I feel as if I were back in Croatia, only now, thank God, I'm on the other side . . .'

'In Croatia, Gian, what on earth did you find in Croatia, a mistress? And my sister, tell me, has she been evacuated too?'

163

Gian strokes his newly growing beard: 'Your sister,' he says, 'has forced others to evacuate, the cow.'

'Explain yourself,' says Pin, acting the buffoon. 'You're offending me, you know.'

'Idiot! Your sister is in the S.S., and wears silk dresses and goes driving round with officers! When the Germans came to the alley, she was the one who led them from house to house, arm-in-arm with a German captain!'

'A captain, Gian! She *has* got on in the world!'

'Are you talking about women informers?' This is said by Cousin, who is thrusting his big face with its flattened nose and its sprouting moustaches towards them.

'Yes, that bitch of a sister of mine,' says Pin. 'She's been a spy and sneak ever since she was a child. What do you expect?'

'Exactly that,' says Cousin, looking into the distance with that disconsolate expression of his, from under the woollen cap.

'It was to be expected of Michel the Frenchman too,' says Gian, 'but he's not really bad, Michel isn't, he's just a rascal.'

'And Pelle, d'you know the new one in the Black Brigade, Pelle?'

'Pelle!' exclaims Gian the driver. 'He's the worst of the lot.'

'He *was* the worst,' says a voice behind them. They turn round; it's Red Wolf arriving, hung all over with weapons and machine-gun belts captured from the Germans. They greet him warmly; everyone is pleased to see Red Wolf again.

'Why, what's happened to Pelle? How did it go?'

Red Wolf says, 'The *Gap* organized it all,' and he begins telling them what happened.

Pelle used sometimes to go and sleep at his own home, and not in barracks. He lived by himself in the attic of a tenement block, where he kept the whole armoury of weapons which he'd managed to lay hands on, for if he'd taken them to barracks he'd have had to share them with his companions. One night Pelle was on his way home, armed as always. A man was following him, dressed in civilian clothes; he was wearing a raincoat and had his hands thrust in his pockets. Pelle felt himself covered by a firearm. 'Better pretend not to notice,' he thought, and went on walking. On the other pavement there was another man he'd never seen before, also in a raincoat, walking along with his hands in his pockets. Pelle turned a corner and the pair turned too. 'I must get home as quickly as possible,' he thought. 'As soon as I reach the street door I'll jump inside and begin firing from behind the doorposts to keep them off.' But beyond the street door, on the pavement, was another man in a raincoat, coming towards him. 'Better let him pass,' thought Pelle. He stopped and the men in the raincoats stopped too, all three of them. The only thing to do was reach the street door as soon as possible. In the entrance, back against the stair rails, were another two men in raincoats, standing there motionless with their hands in their pockets. Pelle had already entered. 'Now they've got me in a trap,' he thought. 'Now they'll say: "Hands up!"' But they did not seem to be looking at him. 'If they still follow me,' he thought, 'I'll turn on the stairs and fire down between the rails.' When he reached the second flight he looked down. They were following; Pelle was still covered by the invisible weapons in the pockets of their raincoats. Another landing; Pelle frowned down. On each flight of stairs below him was a man coming up. Pelle went on climbing, keeping very close to the wall, but at whatever point of the stairs he'd reached, there was always a man of the *Gap*, one or two or three or four flights below him, coming up close to the wall, and keeping him covered. Six floors, seven floors. The well of the staircase in the dim light of the black-out looked like a series of mirrors, with a man in a raincoat repeated numberless times on every flight, spiralling slowly up towards him. 'If they don't fire at me before I reach the attic,' thought Pelle, 'I'm safe; I'll barricade myself inside and I've got enough weapons and grenades there to resist till the Black Brigade arrives.' Now he had reached the last floor under the roof. Pelle ran up the last flight, opened his front door, entered and banged it to behind him. 'I'm safe,' he thought. But on the roof, through the windows of the attic, he saw a man in a raincoat aiming a pistol at him. Pelle raised his hands. The door opened behind him. From the stair rails on the landings all the men in raincoats were aiming pistols at him. Then one of them, no one knows who, fired.

The men, halted at the pass, are all standing round Red Wolf, following the story breathlessly. Red Wolf sometimes exaggerates a little in his stories, but he tells them very well.

One of them says: 'What about you, Red Wolf, which of these men were you?'

Red Wolf smiles, and raises his peaked cap on his head which had been shaved in prison. 'The one on the roof,' he says.

He then describes all the weapons Pelle had collected up there; Stens, tommy-guns, hand grenades, pistols of every make and calibre. There was even a mortar, says Red Wolf.

'Look,' he says, and shows them a pistol and some special hand grenades. 'This is all I took, the *Gap* have less weapons than we have, and need them.'

Pin suddenly remembers his pistol. If Pelle knew the place and went and fetched it, it must have been among those; and now he, Pin, had a right to it, it was his, and no one could take it from him!

'Red Wolf, listen, Red Wolf?' he says, pulling him by the jacket. 'Was there a P.38 among Pelle's pistols?'

'A P.38?' replies the other. 'No, there wasn't a P.38. He had every type in the collection, but not a P.38.' And he goes on describing the variety and rarity of the weapons collected by the maniac Pelle.

'Are you quite sure there wasn't a P.38?' asks Pin. 'Could someone from the *Gap* have taken it?'

'No, no, d'you think I wouldn't have noticed a P.38? We went through them all together.'

Then the pistol must still be buried under the spiders' nests, thinks Pin; it's still mine, Pelle didn't know the place, no one knows that magic place but me. This reassures him greatly. Whatever happens, there are still the spiders' nests and the buried pistol.

It is nearly dawn. The brigade still has many hours of marching in front of it, but the leaders consider that lines of men filing along open paths after sunrise would give away their new positions, and decide to wait until the following night before continuing their march in complete secrecy.

This used to be a frontier area, where for many years the Fascists had been playing at preparing a war which in the end they entered completely unprepared; and the mountains are scattered with a variety of long, low, military buildings. Ferriera now sends orders for the detachments to scatter round these huts to sleep and keep hidden for the whole of the next day, till it is dark or misty enough to start marching again.

Places are assigned to the various units; Dritto's detachment is allotted a small isolated building made of cement, with rings in the walls; it must have been a stable. The men stretch themselves out on a few bits of rotten straw on the floor and close their tired eyes, filled with scenes of battle.

In the morning they find it a nuisance having to stay cooped up in there, and only being able to go out one

167

by one to piss behind a wall; but at least they can rest. They are not allowed to sing, or make any smoke from cooking; down at the bottom of the valley there are villages full of spies, with binoculars trained and ears strained for any sound. The men have to go and cook in shifts at a military kitchen with an underground flue which comes out some way off.

Pin does not know what to do with himself; he has sat down in a patch of sun at the door and taken off his broken boots and now completely heelless socks. He looks at his feet in the sun, rubs his blisters, and takes the dirt from between his toes. Then he searches for lice; a daily round-up is necessary if he is not to end up like Giacinto, poor old Giacinto. But what is the use of catching lice if you're going to die one day, like Giacinto? Perhaps the reason that Giacinto didn't rid himself of them was that he knew he was going to die. Pin is sad. The first time he caught lice in a shirt was with Pietromagro in prison. Pin wishes he were reopening the cobbler's in the alley with Pietromagro. But it must be deserted now, the alley, with everyone run away or taken prisoner or killed, and only that bitch of a sister of his left going round with captains. Pin feels that soon he will find himself abandoned all alone in an unknown world, without any idea where to go. The men of the detachment are an ambiguous, stand-offish lot, like the men of the tavern, though much more fascinating and incomprehensible, with that lust to kill in their eyes, and that bestial coupling in the rhododendrons. The only one he feels at home with is Cousin, nice, big, but ruthless Cousin, but he's not here now; in the morning on waking up Pin found he had gone, with his woollen cap and his tommy-gun, off on one of his mysterious expeditions. And now the detachment will be broken up, too. Kim had said so to Gian the driver. The others know nothing about this so far. Pin turns to them as they lie crowded up against each other on the scanty straw on the cement floor.

'God, if I didn't come and give you news, you wouldn't even know you were born.'

'What's up now? Spit it out,' they say.

'The detachment is to be broken up,' he says, 'as soon as we get to the new area.'

'Sure. Who said so?'

'Kim. I swear.'

Dritto shows no sign of having heard. He knows what this means.

'Don't talk balls, Pin. Where can they send us?'

They begin to discuss the detachments to which the various men could be assigned, and which they would prefer to go to.

'Don't you know they're going to make a special detachment for each, though?' says Pin. 'They'll make all of us commanders. Long Zena they'll make commander of the arm-chair-borne partisans. Sure, a detachment of partisans who go into action sitting down. There are soldiers mounted on horses, aren't there? Now they'll have partisans mounted on rocking-chairs!'

'Wait till I've finished reading,' says Long Zena, holding a finger in his *Super-Thriller* to keep the place. 'Then I'll answer you. I'm just on the point of guessing the murderer.'

'The murderer of the bull?' asks Pin.

Long Zena can no longer follow either his book or the conversation.

'What bull?'

Pin breaks out into one of his high-pitched laughs; Long Zena has fallen into his trap. 'The bull you got the lips from! Bull's-lips! Bull's-lips!'

Long Zena leans over on one of his huge hands to get up,

still keeping his place in the book, and waves the other about in an attempt to grab Pin; then he realizes it's not worth the effort and begins reading again.

The men all laugh at Pin's jokes; they are enjoying this performance; when Pin starts making fun of people he goes right through the lot of them.

Pin, happy and excited, laughs till the tears come into his eyes; he's in his element, now, in among the grown-ups, people who are enemies and friends at the same time, whom he can laugh at till he has vented his hatred for them. He feels ruthless; he'll hurt them without any pity.

Giglia laughs too, but Pin knows that it's a forced laugh; she is frightened. Pin glances at her now and again; she does not lower her eyes, but the smile is trembling on her lips; you wait, thinks Pin, you won't be laughing long.

'Carabiniere!' exclaims Pin. At every new name he brings in, the men give subdued grins, enjoying in anticipation what Pin will come out with.

'Carabiniere will be given a special detachment . . .' begins Pin.

'To keep order with,' says Carabiniere, defensively.

'No, my lad, to arrest parents with!'

Every time Carabiniere is reminded of that business of arresting the conscripts' parents, it makes him furious.

'It's not true! I never arrested any of their parents!'

Pin's voice is full of subdued, concentrated irony; the men are listening with approval, backing him up. 'Now don't get angry, lad, don't get angry. A detachment to arrest parents with . . . You're so good at arresting parents!'

Carabiniere is getting more and more furious; then suddenly he thinks it might be better to let Pin have his say, till he tires and passes on to someone else.

'Now we'll go on to . . .' Pin swivels his eyes round, then

stops with his face set in one of those smiles which bare his gums and cover his eyes with freckles. The men have already guessed who he is referring to, and hold back their laughter. Duke seems almost hypnotized by Pin's grin, his moustache is standing straight up and his cheeks are drawn. 'I'll bbblow your bbballs off, I'll kkkick your arse,' he hisses between his teeth.

'. . . there'll be a special detachment for Duke too . . . to gut rabbits. God, you boast so much, Duke, and I've never seen you do anything more than twist chickens' necks and skin rabbits!'

Duke puts a hand on his Austrian pistol and looks as if he's going to gore him with his fur cap. 'I'll cccut *your* gggguts out!' he shouts.

Then Mancino makes a false move. He says: 'And what shall we put Pin in charge of?'

Pin looks at Mancino as if noticing him for the first time. 'Oh, Mancino, you're back, are you . . . ? You've been away from home so long . . . Lots of exciting things have happened while you were away . . .'

He turns round slowly; Dritto is in a corner, looking serious; Giglia is near the door with that hypocritical smile of hers always on her lips.

'Guess what detachment you'll be in charge of, Mancino . . .'

Mancino gives his sour laugh and tries to forestall him: 'A cooking-pot detachment . . .' he says, and doubles up with laughter, as if he had made the wittiest joke in the world.

Pin shakes his head, with a serious face. Mancino blinks . . . 'a hawk detachment . . .' he says, and tries to laugh again, but only makes a strange sound in his throat.

Pin shakes his head again.

'. . . a naval detachment . . .' says Mancino, and now his mouth has not opened, and there are tears in his eyes.

171

Pin now puts on a clownish, hypocritical expression, and says slowly and unctuously: 'Well, your detachment won't be so very different from others. Except that it'll only be able to move about in the open, along wide roads, and in places where there's nothing growing higher than bushes.'

Mancino begins laughing again, first silently then louder and louder; he has not yet realized what Pin is getting at, but is laughing all the same. The men are now hanging on Pin's every word, some of them have already understood and are grinning.

'It'll be able to go anywhere, except in the woods . . . except where there are branches . . . where there are branches . . .'

'Woods . . . Ha, ha, ha . . . Branches,' laughs Mancino. 'Why though . . . ?'

'It would get stuck . . . your detachment would . . . get stuck by your cuckold's horns!'

The others burst into roars of laughter. The cook gets up, looking sour, his mouth contracted. The laughter dies down a little. The cook looks round, then begins laughing himself again, with swollen eyes and twisted mouth, a forced, savage laugh, and clapping his hands on his knees and pointing to Pin as if to say: 'That's a good one . . .'

'Pin . . . take a look at him . . .' he says, grinning falsely now. 'Pin . . . we'll give him the lavatory detachment, that's what we'll give him . . .'

Dritto has now got up too.

He takes a step or two towards them. 'Stop all this nonsense,' he says sharply. 'Don't you realize you mustn't make any noise?'

It is the first time since the battle that he has given an order. And he gives it on the excuse that they are not supposed to make any noise, instead of saying: 'Stop all this nonsense because I don't like it.'

172

The men give him sour looks; he is no longer their commander, this man.

Giglia's voice is now heard: 'Pin, why don't you sing us a song, instead . . . Sing us the one . . .'

'The lavatory detachment . . .' croaks Mancino. 'With a chamber-pot on your head . . . Ha, ha, ha . . . Pin with a chamber-pot on his head, imagine it . . .'

'What would you like me to sing you, Giglia?' says Pin. 'The same one as last time . . . ?'

'Shut up,' says Dritto. 'Don't you know the orders? Don't you know we're in a danger zone?'

'Sing us that song . . .' says Giglia. 'The one you do so well . . . How does it go? *Oili, Oilà* . . .'

'With a chamber-pot on his head,' the cook is still laughing and clapping his knees, though there are tears of rage at the corners of his eyes. 'And an enema-tube as a gun . . . A burst of enema-tubes, you'll give, Pin . . .'

'*Oili, Oilà*, Giglia, are you sure . . . ?' says Pin. 'I've never heard of any songs that go "*Oili, Oilà*", there aren't any . . .'

'Bursts of enema-tubes . . . Look at him . . . Pin,' croaks the cook.

'*Oili, Oilà*,' Pin begins improvising. 'The husband goes to war, oilir oilor, and leaves his wife at home, oilim oilom!'

'Pin is a little pimp, oilir oilimp!' shouts Mancino, trying to drown Pin's voice.

Dritto sees that for the first time no one is obeying him. He grabs Pin's arm and begins twisting it: 'Shut up! Shut up! D'you understand?'

Pin feels the pain but goes on singing: 'Oiler, oiler, the wife and the commander, oili oiloo, what will he do?' The cook is determined to outdo Pin, refusing to listen to his song: 'Oili, Oilore, you're the brother of a whore!'

Dritto is now twisting both Pin's arms, feeling the little

bones under his fingers; he'll break them in a second, if he goes on. 'Shut up, you little bastard, shut up!'

Pin's eyes are full of tears; he is biting his lips: 'Oili oilo, to the bushes off they go, oili oilogs, like a pair of dogs!'

Dritto drops one of Pin's arms and puts a hand over his mouth. It is a foolish, dangerous thing to do. Pin sinks his teeth into a finger and bites with all his might. Dritto gives a lacerating scream. Pin lets go the finger and looks round. They all have their eyes on him, these incomprehensible enemies the grown-ups: Dritto is sucking his bleeding finger, Mancino is laughing hysterically, Giglia is looking ashen, and all the others are following the scene breathlessly with glittering eyes.

'Swine!' shouts Pin, breaking into sobs. 'Bastards! Bitches!'

The only thing for him now is to escape. Get right away. Pin runs outside.

Dritto is shouting after him: 'No one is to leave the camp! Come back, Pin, come back!' and makes as if to run after him.

But at the door he bumps into two armed men.

'Dritto, we were looking for you.'

Dritto recognizes them. They are two runners from brigade headquarters.

'Kim and Ferriera want to see you. To report. Come with us.'

Dritto becomes impassive again. 'Let's go,' he says, and picks up his tommy-gun.

'Unarmed, they said,' the men explain.

Dritto does not flicker an eyelid; he takes the strap off his shoulder.

'Let's go,' he says.

'And the pistol too,' say the men.

Dritto loosens his belt and lets the pistol fall to the ground.

'Let's go,' he says.

Now he is standing between the two men.

He turns round: 'Our turn to fetch the rations is at two o'clock. Begin getting everything ready. At half-past three, two of our men must go on sentry duty, beginning from where the last night's roster broke off.'

He turns round again and walks off between the two men.

CHAPTER TWELVE

Pin is sitting all alone on a mountain crest; sheer away at his feet drop rocky slopes furry with bushes, and then valley folding into valley down to where black rivers coil in the depths. Long wisps of cloud are moving up the slopes and blotting out the scattered villages and trees.

This is something irreparable now – as irreparable as when he stole the pistol from the sailor, or left the men in the tavern, or escaped from prison. Never again will he be able to return to the detachment, never will he be able to go into action with them now. It is sad to be like him, a child in a world of grown-ups, always treated as an amusement or a nuisance; and never to be able to use those exciting and mysterious things, weapons and women, never to be able to take part in their games. But one day Pin will be grown-up too, and be able to behave really badly to everyone, revenge himself on those who have behaved badly to him; how Pin would like to be grown-up now, or rather not grown-up, but remain as he is, yet admired and feared, a child and yet a leader of grown-ups on some marvellous enterprise.

Now he will leave these windswept unknown parts and go far away, back to his own kingdom in the river-bed, back to the magic spot where the spiders make their nests. Down there his pistol is buried, with that mysterious name; pee thirty-eight. With his pistol Pin will become a partisan all on his own, with no one to twist his arm till it nearly breaks, no one to send him off to bury dead hawks so that a man and woman can roll about together among rhododendrons. He will do wonderful things, will Pin, always on his own; kill an officer, a captain, the captain who goes round with that bitch and spy of a sister. Then he will be respected by all the grown-ups, and they will want him to go into action with them; perhaps they will teach him how to handle a machine-gun. And Giglia will no longer say: 'Sing us a song, Pin,' just so that she can snuggle up against her lover; Giglia won't have lovers any more, and one day she will let her breast be touched by him, by Pin, that warm pink breast under her man's shirt.

Now Pin is walking with long strides along the paths winding down the mountainside from the Pass of the Half-Moon; he has a long way to go. And as he walks along he begins to feel that his enthusiasm for those projects was forced, not genuine at all, that they were just fantasies which would never come about in reality, and that he would go on being a poor lost wandering child forever.

Pin walks for the whole day long. He passes places where lovely games could be played, with big white stones to jump about on and twisted trees to climb; he sees squirrels on the tops of pine-trees, snakes winding through the undergrowth, all good targets for stones. But Pin feels no desire to play any games, and goes on walking as hard as he can go, with the sadness clouding in his throat.

He passes a cottage and stops to ask for something to eat. It is inhabited by a little old couple who live on their own and keep goats. The two old folk greet him kindly, offer him chestnuts and milk, and talk about their sons who are all prisoners-of-war far away; then they sit round the fire and begin saying the Rosary, asking Pin to join in too.

But Pin is not used to dealing with people who are good and feels ill at ease – nor is he used to saying the Rosary; so while the old couple are murmuring away with closed eyes he quietly gets down from his chair and goes off.

That night he digs himself a hole in a haystack and sleeps in it; in the morning he presses on, into areas that are becoming more dangerous, infested by Germans. But Pin realizes how useful it sometimes is to be a child, and how no one would believe him even if he said quite openly that he was a partisan.

At one point he finds the way barred by a road-block. From some way off he can see Germans frowning at him under their helmets. Pin goes boldly up to them.

'My sheep,' he says. 'Have you seen my sheep?'

'*Was?*' The Germans can't understand.

'Sheep. She-e-e-p. Ba-a-a-a-a . . .'

The Germans laugh; they have understood. With that long hair and all wrapped up as he is, Pin might easily be a little shepherd-boy.

'I've lost a sheep,' he whines. 'It must have passed this way, for sure. Where's it gone to?' And Pin nips under the barrier and walks on, calling out, 'Ba-a-a-a . . .' He's got away with that too.

The sea, which yesterday looked just a turbid mass of cloud on the edge of the sky, is now becoming a darkening strip of colour and then a great blue background to the hills and houses.

Pin reaches his own river-bed. It's an evening with very few frogs about. Black tadpoles are setting the water in the puddles aquiver. There, beyond the bamboos, begins the path of the spiders' nests, the magic place which only Pin knows. There

177

he can weave strange spells, become a king, a god. He starts walking up the path, his heart in his mouth. Yes, there are the nests. But the earth is disturbed, some hand seems to have passed over it all, tearing up the grass, moving the stones, destroying the nests and breaking open the walls of chewed grass; Pelle! Pelle knew the place; he's been here, with those lips of his slobbering with rage, scooped the loose earth out with his saliva-flecked hands and nails, pushed sticks into the tunnels and killed all the spiders one by one, looking for the pee thirty-eight pistol! Did he find it? Pin can no longer recognize the hiding-place; the stones he had laid are no longer there, the grass is torn out in handfuls. This should be the place though, the hole he scooped out for it is still there, but now it's full of earth and bits of stone.

Pin puts his head in his hands and sobs. No one will ever give him his pistol back now. Pelle is dead and did not have it among his weapons; where could he have put it, who could he have given it to? The pistol was the last thing Pin had in all the world; what is he to do now? He can't go back to the partisans; he has behaved too badly to all of them, Mancino, Giglia, Duke, Long Zena. There has been a round-up at the tavern and everyone there has been deported or killed. The only one left is Michel the Frenchman, in the Black Brigade. But Pin does not want to end up like Pelle, climbing up a long staircase waiting to be shot at. He is alone in all the world, is Pin.

The Dark Girl of Long Alley is trying on a new blue dressing-gown, when she hears a knock at the door. She listens; these days she is afraid of opening her door to people she doesn't know, when she's in her old home in the alley. There's another knock.

'Who's there?'

'Open up, Rina. It's your brother, Pin.'

178

Rina opens the door and her brother comes in, dressed in strange clothes, with a shock of hair wider than his shoulders, filthy, ragged, his boots falling to bits, his cheeks clotted with dust and tears.

'Pin! Where on earth have you come from? Where have you been all this time?'

Pin enters without looking at her, and says hoarsely: 'Now don't start annoying me. Where I've been is my business. Have you made anything to eat?'

The Dark Girl becomes all maternal: 'Wait a minute and I'll get something ready. Sit down. How tired you must be, poor Pin. You're lucky to have found me at home. I'm scarcely ever here nowadays. I live at the hotel now.'

Pin begins chewing bread and a piece of German hazelnut chocolate.

'They treat you well, I see.'

'Pin, I've been so worried about you! What have you been doing all this time? Being a vagabond, a rebel?'

'And what about you?' asks Pin.

The Dark Girl is spreading slices of bread with German malt spread and passing them to him.

'And what are you going to do now, Pin?'

'I don't know. Let me eat.'

'Look here, Pin, you must try and be sensible. You know, at the place I work they need bright lads like you and could look after you well. There's no real work; just going round all day, watching people.'

'Say, Rina, have you any weapons?'

'Me?'

'Yes, you.'

'Well, I've got a pistol. I keep it with me because one never knows these days. Someone from the Black Brigade gave it to me.'

179

Pin raises his eyes and swallows down the last mouthful. 'Will you show it to me, Rina?'

The Dark Girl gets up. 'Why are you so obsessed with pistols? Didn't you have enough of them when you stole Frick's? This one is just like Frick's. Here it is. Poor Frick, they've sent him over to the Atlantic coast.'

Pin looks at the pistol, fascinated. It's a pee thirty-eight. His pee thirty-eight!

'Who gave it to you?'

'I told you, someone in the Black Brigade. A blond boy; he had such a cold. And without exaggeration he must have had at least seven different pistols on him. "What d'you do with so many?" I asked. "Give me one," I said. But he didn't want to, however much I begged him. A mania for pistols, he had. Finally he gave me this one because it was in the worst condition. But it works all the same. "What's this you're giving me," I said, "a cannon?" And he said, "Well, this way it stays in the family." God knows what he meant.'

Pin is not even listening any more; he is turning his pistol over and over in his hand. Then he raises his eyes to his sister, hugging the pistol to his chest as if it were a doll, and says hoarsely, 'Listen to me, Rina, this pistol's mine!'

The Dark Girl gives him a black look. 'What's got hold of you? Have you become a rebel?'

Pin takes up a chair and flings it on the ground.

'Cow!' he shouts with all his strength. 'Bitch! Spy!'

He thrusts the pistol into a pocket and bangs the door on his way out.

Outside it is already night. The alley is deserted, like when he came. The shutters of the shops are up. There are shrapnel shelters against the walls, made of planks and sand-bags.

Pin takes the path to the river-bed. He feels as if he were

back at that night when he stole the pistol. Now he has his pistol, but everything is just as it was; he is alone in all the world, and lonelier than ever. And Pin's heart is overflowing with a single question, as it was that night: 'What shall I do?'

He walks along the irrigation channels, weeping. First he cries silently then breaks out into loud sobs. There is no one to come towards him now, as there was before. No one? A big shadow of a man is falling on a turn of the channel.

'Cousin!'

'Pin!'

These are enchanted places, where magical things always happen. The pistol is enchanted too, like a magic wand. And Cousin is also like a great magician, with his tommy-gun and his woollen cap, as he pats Pin's head and asks: 'Well, Pin, what are you doing down here?'

'I came to fetch my pistol. Look. A German naval pistol.'

Cousin looks at it closely.

'Lovely. A P.38. Look after it carefully.'

'And you, what are you doing here, Cousin?'

Cousin sighs, with that eternally regretful air of his, as if he were always undergoing some punishment.

'I'm going to pay a visit,' he says.

'These places are mine, down here. Magic places. Spiders make their nests here.'

'Do spiders make nests, Pin?'

'This is the only place in the whole world where they do,' explains Pin, 'and I'm the only person who knows it. Then that Fascist Pelle came and mucked everything up. Would you like me to show you?'

'Yes, show me, Pin. Spiders' nests, just fancy.'

Pin takes him by his big hand, soft and warm as bread.

'There, you see, here there were lots of doors into their

little tunnels. That Fascist swine broke them all up. Here is a complete one still, d'you see?'

Cousin has knelt down nearby and is peering into the darkness. 'My goodness you're right, a little door that opens and shuts. And a tunnel inside. Is it deep?'

'Very deep,' explains Pin, 'with bits of chewed grass stuck all round the sides. The spider is at the end.'

'Let's light a match,' says Cousin.

They both kneel down, side by side, watching the mouth of the tunnel by the light of the match.

'Here, throw the match inside,' says Pin, 'let's see if the spider comes out.'

'Why, poor little thing?' says Cousin. 'Don't you see how much harm has been done to them already?'

'Say, Cousin, d'you think they'll remake their nests?'

'Yes, I think so, if we leave them in peace.'

'Shall we come back another time and see?'

'Yes, Pin, we'll pass by this way every month and have a look.'

How wonderful it is to have found Cousin, who is interested in spiders' nests.

'Say, Pin.'

'Yes, Cousin?'

'Say, Pin, there's something I want to tell you. I know you understand these things. You see, it's months and months since I've been with a woman . . . You understand these things, Pin. Listen, they say that your sister . . .'

Pin is grinning his old grin; he is the grown-ups' friend, is Pin; yes, he understands these things and is proud to oblige his friends in this way when he can. 'Hell, Cousin, you'll be all right with my sister. I'll show you the way. D'you know Long Alley? Well, it's the door after the boiler-repairer's, on the first landing. Don't worry, you won't meet anyone in the street. But be a bit careful with her. Don't say who you are, nor that I sent you. Tell her you work at the "Todt" and are just passing through. Ha, Cousin, yet you're always saying such awful things about women. Go on, then, she's a big brunette, my sister is, and men like her a lot.'

A slight smile passes over Cousin's big disconsolate features.

'Thank you, Pin. You're a real friend. I'll be back soon.'

'God, Cousin, are you taking your tommy-gun with you?'

Cousin runs a finger over his moustaches.

'Well, you see, I don't like going around unarmed.'

Cousin seems so embarrassed about this that it makes Pin laugh. 'Here, take my pistol. Leave me the tommy-gun and I'll keep guard over it.'

Cousin puts down the tommy-gun, thrusts the pistol into his pocket, then takes off his woollen cap and puts that into his pocket too. Then he tries to tidy his hair with two fingers wet with spittle.

'You're making yourself look your best, I see, Cousin. You want to make an impression. Be quick, now, if you want to find her at home.'

'See you soon, Pin,' says Cousin, and off he goes.

Now Pin is alone in the darkness, by the spiders' nests, with the tommy-gun on the ground near him. But he is no longer in despair. He has found Cousin, and Cousin is the great friend he has sought for so long, the friend who is interested in spiders' nests. Yet Cousin is like all other grown-ups, with that mysterious desire for women, and now he has gone to visit his sister and is embracing her on the unmade bed. Thinking it over, Pin decides that it would have been nicer if Cousin had not thought of that, and had stayed there with him instead looking at the spiders' nests a little longer, and made his usual remarks against women which Pin approved

183

and understood so perfectly. Instead of which Cousin is like all other grown-ups; there's nothing to be done about it, Pin understands these things.

Shots, down in the Old Town. Who can it be? Patrols, perhaps, on their rounds. Shots, at night like that, are always frightening. Cousin was really rather rash to go alone into that nest of Fascists, just for a woman. Pin is worried he may fall into the hands of a patrol, or find his sister's room full of Germans and get captured. Deep down, though, Pin feels that would be only just and he would be happy at that. What pleasure can he get from going with that hairy frog of a sister of his?

But if Cousin is captured, Pin would be all alone, alone with that tommy-gun which frightens him and he doesn't know how to handle. He hopes Cousin won't be captured, he hopes it with all his might, not because Cousin is the Great Friend he was looking for, no, he's not that any more, he's just a man like all the others, but because he is the last person Pin has left in all the world.

However, there's still a long time to go before he need start worrying. Instead of which he now sees a shadow coming nearer, and there he is already.

'How on earth were you so quick, Cousin, have you already done it?'

Cousin shakes his head with that disconsolate air of his.

'No. You know, I got disgusted and came away without doing anything.'

'Hell, Cousin, you got disgusted?'

Pin is delighted. He really is the Great Friend, Cousin is.

Cousin puts the tommy-gun back on his shoulder and hands the pistol back to Pin.

They walk off into the country, with Pin holding Cousin's big soft calming hand, a hand as comforting as bread.

The darkness is punctured with tiny spots of light; numberless fireflies are flickering over the hedges.

'Filthy creatures, women, Cousin . . .' says Pin.

'All of them . . .' agrees Cousin. 'But they weren't always; now my mother . . .'

'Can you remember your mother, then?' asks Pin.

'Yes, she died when I was fifteen,' says Cousin.

'Was she nice?'

'Yes,' says Cousin, 'she was nice.'

'Mine was nice too,' says Pin.

'What a lot of fireflies,' says Cousin.

'If you look at them really closely, the fireflies,' says Pin, 'they're filthy creatures too, all reddish in colour.'

'Yes,' says Cousin, 'but seen from this distance they're beautiful.'

And they walk on, the big man and the child, into the night, amid the fireflies, holding each other by the hand.

PENGUIN MODERN CLASSICS

THE ROAD TO SAN GIOVANNI
ITALO CALVINO

'Brimming with Calvino's beautifully crafted prose, dry humour and continual questioning of his own writing and memory' *Observer*

The Road to San Giovanni contains five autobiographical essays – fascinating expeditions through the memories of one of the greatest writers of the twentieth century. In these elegant meditations Calvino delves into his past, remembering awkward childhood walks with his father, a lifelong obsession with the cinema and fighting in the Italian Resistance against the Fascists. He also muses on the social contract, language and sensations associated with emptying the kitchen rubbish and the shape he would, if asked, consider the world. These reflections on the nature of memory itself are engaging, witty and lit through with Calvino's alchemical brilliance.

'Urbane and always elegant ... shows us what a master we have lost in Italo Calvino' *Literary Review*

*Contemporary ... Provocative ... Outrageous ...
Prophetic ... Groundbreaking ... Funny ... Disturbing ...
Different ... Moving ... Revolutionary ... Inspiring ...
Subversive ... Life-changing ...*

What makes a modern classic?

At Penguin Classics our mission has always been to make the best
books ever written available to everyone. And that also means
constantly redefining and refreshing exactly what makes a 'classic'.
That's where Modern Classics come in. Since 1961 they have been an
organic, ever-growing and ever-evolving list of books from the last
hundred (or so) years that we believe will continue to be read over and
over again.

They could be books that have inspired political dissent, such as
Animal Farm. Some, like *Lolita* or *A Clockwork Orange*, may have
caused shock and outrage. Many have led to great films, from *In Cold
Blood* to *One Flew Over the Cuckoo's Nest*. They have broken down
barriers – whether social, sexual, or, in the case of *Ulysses*, the
boundaries of language itself. And they might – like *Goldfinger* or
Scoop – just be pure classic escapism. Whatever the reason, Penguin
Modern Classics continue to inspire, entertain and enlighten millions
of readers everywhere.

'No publisher has had more influence on reading habits than Penguin'
Independent

'Penguins provided a crash course in world literature'
Guardian

The best books ever written

PENGUIN (🐧) CLASSICS

SINCE 1946

Find out more at www.penguinclassics.com